INTERWORLD

Other Books for Young Readers by

NEIL GAIMAN

Coraline

The Wolves in the Walls

The Day I Swapped My Dad for Two Goldfish

MirrorMask

INTER

WORLD

NEIL GAIMAN
MICHAEL REAVES

eos *An Imprint of* HarperCollins*Publishers*

Eos is an imprint of HarperCollins Publishers.

InterWorld
Copyright © 2007 by Neil Gaiman and Michael Reaves
All rights reserved. Printed in the United States of America.
No part of this book may be used or reproduced in any manner
whatsoever without written permission except in the case of brief
quotations embodied in critical articles and reviews.
For information address HarperCollins Children's Books,
a division of HarperCollins Publishers,
1350 Avenue of the Americas, New York, NY 10019.
ISBN 978-0-06-123896-3
Typography by Hilary Zarycky

Neil would like to dedicate this book to his son Mike, who read the manuscript and liked it and encouraged us, and always asked when he was going to be able to read it in a real book.

Michael would like to dedicate this book to Steve Saffel.

AUTHORS' NOTE

This is a work of fiction. Still, given an infinite number of possible worlds, it must be true on one of them. And if a story set in an infinite number of possible universes is true in one of them, then it must be true in all of them. So maybe it's not as fictional as we think.

INTERWORLD

PART I

CHAPTER ONE

Once I got lost in my own house.

I guess it wasn't quite as bad as it sounds. We had just built a new annex—added a hallway and a bedroom for the squid, aka Kevin, my really little brother—but still, the carpenters had left and the dust had settled over a month ago. Mom had just sounded the dinner call and I was on my way downstairs. I took a wrong turn on the second floor and found myself in a room wallpapered with clouds and bunnies. I realized I'd turned right instead of left, so I promptly made the same mistake again and blundered into the closet.

By the time I got downstairs Jenny and Dad were already there and Mom was giving me the Look. I knew trying to explain would sound lame, so I just clammed up and dug in to my mac and cheese.

But you see the problem. I don't have what my aunt Maude used to call a "bump of direction." If anything, I've got a hollow where the bump should be. Forget knowing north from south or east from west—I have a hard enough time telling right from left. Which is all pretty ironic, considering how things turned out . . .

But I'm getting ahead of myself. Okay. I'm going to write this like Mr. Dimas taught us. He said it doesn't matter where you start, as long as you start somewhere. So I'm going to start with him.

It was the end of the October term of my sophomore year, and everything was pretty normal, except for Social Studies, which was no big surprise. Mr. Dimas, who taught the class, had a reputation for unconventional teaching methods. For midterms he had blindfolded us, then had us each stick a pin in a map of the world and we got to write essays on wherever the pin stuck. I got Decatur, Illinois. Some of the guys complained because they drew places like Ulan Bator or Zimbabwe. They were lucky. *You* try writing ten thousand words on Decatur, Illinois.

But Mr. Dimas was always doing stuff like that. He made the front page of the local paper last year and nearly got fired when he turned two classes into warring fiefdoms that tried to negotiate peace for an entire semester. The peace talks eventually broke down and the two classes went to war on the quad during free period. Things got a little carried away and a few bloody noses resulted. Mr. Dimas was quoted on the local news as saying, "Sometimes war is necessary to teach us the value of peace. Sometimes you need to learn the real value of diplomacy in avoiding war. And I'd rather my students learned those lessons on the playground than on the battlefield."

Rumor at school was that he was going to be canned for that one. Even Mayor Haenkle was pretty annoyed, seeing as how his son's nose was one of the ones bloodied. Mom and Jenny—my younger sister—and I sat up late, drinking Ovaltine and waiting for Dad to come home from the city council meeting. The squid was fast asleep in Mom's lap— she was still breast-feeding him back then. It was after midnight when Dad came in the back door, tossed his hat on the table and said, "The vote was seven to six, in favor. Dimas keeps his job. My throat's sore."

Mom got up to fix Dad some tea, and Jenny asked Dad why he'd gone to bat for Mr. Dimas. "My teacher says he's a troublemaker."

"He is," Dad said. "—Thanks, hon." He sipped the tea, then went on. "He's also one of the few teachers around who actually cares about what he's doing, and who has more than a spoonful of brains to do it with." He pointed his pipe at Jenny and said, "Past the witching hour, sprite. You belong in bed."

That was how Dad was. Even though he's just a city councilman, he has more sway among some people than the mayor does. Dad used to be a Wall Street broker, and he still handles stocks for a few of Greenville's more prominent citizens, including several on the school board. The councilman job takes only a few days a month most of the year, so Dad drives a cab most days. I asked him once why he did it,

5

since his investments keep the wolf from the door even without Mom's home jewelry business, and he said he liked meeting new people.

You'd think that nearly getting fired might've thrown a scare into Mr. Dimas and gotten him to back off a little, but no such luck. His idea for this year's Social Studies final was pretty extreme even for him. He divided our class into ten teams of three each, blindfolded us again—he was big on blindfolds—and had a school bus drop us off at random places in the city. We were supposed to find our way to various checkpoints within a certain time without maps. One of the other teachers asked what this had to do with Social Studies, and Mr. Dimas said that everything was Social Studies. He confiscated all cell phones, phone cards, credit cards and cash so we couldn't call for rides or take buses or cabs. We were on our own.

And that was where it all began.

It's not like we were in any real danger—downtown Greenville isn't downtown LA or New York or even downtown Decatur, Illinois. The worst that might happen would be an old lady clobbering us with her purse if one of us was foolish enough to try to help her across 42nd Avenue. Still, I was partnered with Rowena Danvers and Ted Russell, which meant that this was going to be interesting.

The school bus pulled away in a cloud of diesel smoke and

we took our blindfolds off. We were downtown—that much was obvious. It was the middle of the day, a chilly October afternoon. Traffic, both foot and car, was pretty light. I immediately looked for the street sign, which said we were on the corner of Sheckley Boulevard and Simak Street.

And I knew where we were.

This was such a surprise that I was tongue-tied for a moment. I was the kid who could get lost going to the corner mailbox, but I knew where this was—we were standing right across the street and down the block from the dentist, where Jenny and I had both had our teeth cleaned just a couple of days before.

Before I could say anything, Ted pulled out the card Mr. Dimas had given each of us on which was written the location where we were to be picked up. "We have to get to the corner of Maple and Whale," he said. "Hey, maybe we can get your dad to pick us up, Harker."

This is all you have to know about Ted Russell: He wouldn't be able spell "IQ." Not because he's dumb—which he is, as a bag of rocks—but because he couldn't be bothered. He was a year older than me, due to having been kept back. I knew I would get nothing but the kind of jokes even grade-schoolers would roll their eyes at from him. But I was willing to put up with Russell, obnoxious jerk that he was, to be here—to be anywhere—with Rowena Danvers.

I suppose there may have been prettier, smarter, just

generally nicer girls at Greenville High, but I'd never bothered looking for them. As far as I was concerned, Rowena was the only girl for me. But after two years of trying, I had failed to convince Rowena that I was anything more than a minor extra in the movie of her life. It wasn't that she hated me, or even disliked me—I wasn't important enough to warrant that. I doubt that we'd exchanged more than five sentences during the entire school year, and probably four of those five were along the lines of "Excuse me, but you dropped this" or "I'm sorry, were you sitting here?" Not exactly the stuff of which great romances are made, although I treasured every one of them.

But now, just maybe, I could change that. I could become more than an anonymous blip on her radar. I was practically fifteen, and she was my honest-to-goodness First Love. I mean it. Or I thought I did at the time. It wasn't just a crush. I wasn't simply in love with Rowena Danvers—I was madly, deeply, *passionately* in love. I even told my parents how I felt, and that took guts. If she ever noticed me, I said to them, this would be one of the great love affairs of the century. They could see I was serious, and they didn't even tease me. They got it. They wished me luck. I would be Tristran and she would be Iseult (whoever they were; that was what Dad said); I would be Sid and she would be Nancy (whoever they were; that was what Mom said). I wanted to impress Rowena Danvers, and so what if demonstrating that I knew how to cross a street in the right direction wasn't exactly the stuff that Shakespeare was made of? I'd take what I could get.

I said, "I know where we are."

Ted and Rowena looked at me dubiously. "Yeah, right. I'd sooner put the blindfold back on. Come on, Rowena," Ted said, taking her arm. "Everybody knows that Harker couldn't find his butt with both hands tied behind him."

She pulled her arm free and looked at me. I could see that she didn't relish walking five or six blocks with Ted Russell, but that she also didn't want to be wandering around downtown for the rest of the day. "Are you *sure* you know where we are, Joey?" she asked.

The woman I loved was asking me for help! I felt like I could have found my way home from the dark side of the moon. "No problem," I said with all the confidence of a lemming who thinks he's headed for a nice day at the seashore. "Follow me. Come on!" And I started down the street.

Rowena hesitated a moment more, then turned away from Ted and started walking after me. He stared after her in shock for a moment, then waved his arm in a "g'wan!" gesture. "Your funeral. I'll tell Dimas to send out search parties," he shouted, then he laughed and pumped the air.

It must be nice to be your own audience.

Rowena caught up with me, and we walked on for a while in silence. We crossed Arkwright Park and headed north—I think—on Corinth.

Within six blocks I realized something very important: It's good to know where you are, but it's better to know *where you're going*. Which I definitely did not—in a matter of minutes I was more lost than I've ever been. And, what was worse, Rowena knew it. I could tell by the way she was looking at me.

I was starting to panic. I didn't want to let Rowena down. But I also didn't want her to see me with egg on my face. So I said, "Wait here just a minute," and I ran on ahead before she could say anything.

I was desperately hoping to find another street or landmark that I recognized. I turned the corner and saw a building at the end of the next block that looked familiar, so I started down the street—Arkwright Boulevard, next to the park—to make sure.

The weather in Greenville is weird at the best of times. It comes of being so close to the Grand River, which gave us the beer-brewing industry and the tourists who come down to walk the nature trail and to see the falls, but also gives us the mists that spread around the town whenever it gets chilly.

One of those mists started at the corner of Arkwright and Corinth. I headed straight into it, felt it beading cold on my face. Most mists thin when you're in them. This one didn't.

It was more like walking through thick smoke, blinding and gray.

I just pushed through it, not really noticing it much—after all, I had more important things on my mind. From the inside of the mist I could see shimmering lights of all different colors. It's weird what a town looks like when all you can see are the lights.

I turned the next corner onto Fallbrook and stepped out of the mist—and stopped. I was in a part of town I didn't recognize at all. Across the street was a McDonald's I'd never seen before, with a huge green tartan arch above it. Some kind of Scottish promotion, I guessed. Weird. I noticed it, but it didn't really register. I was too busy thinking about Rowena, and wondering whether there was any way to explain what had happened that wouldn't leave her thinking I was a complete idiot. There wasn't. I was going to have to head back to her and confess that I had gotten us both completely lost. I was looking forward to it about the same way I look forward to a routine dental checkup.

At least the fog was almost gone when I got back to the cross street, panting and out of breath. Rowena was still waiting where I had left her. She was staring into the window of a pet shop, with her back to me. I ran straight across the street, tapped Rowena on the shoulder and said, "I'm sorry. Guess we should have listened to Ted. That's not something you hear often, is it?"

She turned around.

When I was a kid—I mean, just a little kid, back in New York, back before we moved to Greenville, before Jenny even—I remember following my mom through Macy's. She was doing her Christmas shopping, and I could have sworn that I barely took my eyes off her. She was wearing a blue coat. I followed her all around the store until the press of people scared me and I grabbed her hand. And she looked down. . . .

And it wasn't my mom at all. It was some woman I'd never seen before, who was wearing a similar blue coat and had the same hairstyle. I started crying and they took me off to some office and gave me a soda and found my mom and it all ended happily enough. But I've never forgotten that moment of dislocation, of expecting one person and seeing another.

That was what I was feeling now. Because it wasn't Rowena in front of me. It looked like her, as much as a sister might, and her clothes were the same. She was even wearing a black baseball cap, just like Rowena's.

But Rowena had always been real vain about her long blond hair. She'd said more than once that she wanted to let it grow as long as it could and never cut it.

This girl wore her blond hair in a buzz cut—*real* short. And she didn't even look like Rowena. Not really. Not when you were up close. Rowena's eyes are blue. This girl had brown eyes. She was just some girl in a brown coat and a black baseball cap, looking at puppies in a pet store window. I was totally confused. I backed away. "I'm sorry," I said. "I thought you were someone else."

She was looking at me like I had just climbed out of the sewer wearing a hockey mask and carrying a chain saw. She didn't say anything.

"Look, I'm really sorry," I told her. "My bad. Okay?"

She nodded without saying anything, and she walked away down the sidewalk until she reached the cross street, glancing behind her every few moments. Then she ran as if all the hounds of hell were after her.

I wanted to apologize for spooking her, but I had my own problems.

I was lost in downtown Greenville. I had gotten separated from the other two members of my unit. I had surrendered all my change. I'd failed Social Studies.

There was only one thing to do, so I did it.

I took off my shoe.

Under the inner sole was a folded five dollar bill. My mom makes me keep it there for emergencies. I took out the five bucks, put my shoe back on, got some change and got on a bus for home, rehearsing all the things I could say to Mr. Dimas, to Rowena, even to Ted, and wondering whether I'd get lucky in the next twelve hours and somehow manage to contract a disease so contagious that they'd have to keep me out of school until the end of the semester. . . .

I knew that my troubles wouldn't be over once I got home. But at least I wouldn't be lost anymore.

As it turned out, I didn't even know the meaning of the word.

CHAPTER TWO

I rode the bus home in a daze. A few blocks after getting on, I stopped looking out the window and started looking at the back of the seat in front of me. Because the streets didn't look right. At first there was nothing specific I could point out that bothered me; everything just seemed a little bit . . . off. Like the green tartan McDonald's arches. I wished I'd heard about whatever they were promoting.

And the cars. Dad says that when he was a kid, he and his friends could easily tell a Ford from a Chevy from a Buick. These days they all look the same no matter who makes them, but it was as if someone had decided that all cars needed to be painted in bright colors—all oranges and leaf greens and cheerful yellows. I didn't see a black car or a silver one all the way.

A cop car went past us, siren on, lights flashing: green and yellow, not red and blue.

After that, I kept my eyes on the gray cracked leather in front of me. About halfway to my street I became obsessed with the idea that my house wouldn't be there, that there would be just an empty lot or—and this was even more disturbing—a *different* house. Or that if there were people there, they wouldn't be my parents and my sister and baby brother. They'd be strangers. I wouldn't belong there anymore.

I got off the bus and ran the three blocks to my house. It looked the same from the outside—same color, same flower beds and window boxes, same wind chimes hanging from the front porch roof. I nearly cried with relief. All of reality might be falling apart around me, but home was still a haven.

I pushed the front door open and went in.

It smelled like my house, not someone else's. Finally I was able to relax.

It looked the same inside as well—but then, as I stood in the hallway, I started to notice things. Little things, subtle things. The kind of things you think that you could be imagining. I thought maybe the hall carpet was a slightly different pattern, but who the heck remembers a carpet pattern? On the living room wall, where there had once been a photo of me in kindergarten, was now a picture of a girl around my age. She looked a little like me—but then, my parents had been talking about getting a photograph of Jenny. . . .

And then it hit me. It was like the time I went over the falls last year, when the barrel hit the rocks and smashed, and suddenly the world was all bright and upside down, and I *hurt*. . . .

There *was* a difference. One you couldn't see from the

front. The annex we'd had built this spring—the new bedroom for Kevin, my baby brother—wasn't there.

I looked up the stairs—if I stood on tiptoe and twisted my neck to just short of painful, I could see where the new hallway started. I tried doing that. I even took a couple of steps up the stairs to see better.

It was no use. The new addition still *wasn't there*.

If this is a joke, I thought, *it's being pulled by a multimillionaire with a really sick sense of humor.*

I heard a noise behind me. I turned around, and there was Mom.

Only she wasn't.

Like Rowena, she looked different. She was wearing jeans and a T-shirt I'd never seen before. Her hair was cut the same as always, but her glasses were different. Like I said, little things.

Except the artificial arm. That wasn't a little thing.

It was made of plastic and metal, and it started just below the sleeve of her T-shirt. She noticed me staring at it, and her look of surprise—she didn't recognize me any more than Rowena had—turned suspicious.

"Who are you? What are you doing in this house?"

By this time I didn't know whether to laugh, cry or start screaming. "Mom," I said desperately, "don't you know me? I'm Joey!"

"Joey?" she said. "I'm not your mom, kid. I don't know

anyone named Joey."

I couldn't say anything to that. I just stared at her. Before I could think of what to say or do, I heard another voice behind me. A girl's voice.

"Mom? Is anything wrong?"

I turned around. I think I was already sort of subconsciously expecting what I would see. Something in the voice told me who would be standing there at the top of the stairs.

It was the girl in the picture.

It wasn't Jenny. This girl had red-brown hair, freckles, kind of a goofy expression, like she spent too much time inside her own head. She was as old as me, so she couldn't be my sister. She looked like—and then I admitted to myself what I already knew—she looked like what I would look like if I were a girl.

We both stared at each other in shock. Faintly, as if from far away, I heard her mother say, "Go back upstairs, Josephine. Hurry."

Josephine.

It was then that I understood, somehow. I don't know how, but it hit me and I knew it was the truth.

I didn't exist anymore. Somehow I'd been *edited out* of my own life. It hadn't worked, obviously, since I was still here. But apparently I was the only one who felt I had any right to be here. Somehow reality had changed so that now Mr. and Mrs. Harker's oldest child was a girl, not a boy. Josephine, not Joseph.

Mrs. Harker—strange to think of her that way—Mrs. Harker was scrutinizing me. She was wary, but she also seemed curious. Well, sure—she was seeing the family resemblance in my face.

"Do I—know you?" She frowned, trying to place me. In another minute she'd figure out why I looked so familiar—she'd remember that I'd called her "Mom"—and, like me, her world would fall apart.

She wasn't my mother. No matter how much I wanted her to be, no matter how much I *needed* her to be, this woman wasn't Mom any more than the woman in the blue coat that day at Macy's.

I ran.

To this day I don't know if I ran away because it was all too much to handle or because I wanted to spare her what I knew: that reality can splinter like a hammered mirror. That it can happen to anybody, because it had just happened to her—and to me.

I ran past her, out of the house, down the street, and I kept running. Maybe I was hoping that if I ran fast enough, far enough, I could somehow go back in time, back to before all this insanity happened. I don't know if it might've worked. I never got a chance to find out.

Suddenly the air in front of me *rippled*. It shimmered, like heat waves gone all silvery, and then it *tore* open. It was like reality itself had split apart. I caught a glimpse of a weird psychedelic background inside, all floating geometric shapes and pulsing colors.

Then through it stepped this—*thing*.

Maybe it was a man—I didn't know. It was wearing a trench coat and hat. I could see the face under the hat brim as it raised its head to look at me.

It had my face.

CHAPTER THREE

The stranger was wearing a full-face mask of some kind, and the surface of it was mirrored, like mercury. It was the strangest thing, staring into that blank, silvery face and seeing my own face staring back at me, all bent and distorted.

My face looked goofy and dumb. A liquid map of freckles, a loose mop of reddish-brown hair, big brown eyes and my mouth twisted into a cartoonish mixture of surprise and, frankly, fear.

The first thing I thought was that the stranger was a robot, one of those liquid metal robots from the movies. Then I thought it was an alien. And then I began to suspect that it was someone I knew wearing some kind of a cool high-tech mask, and it was that thought that grew into a certainty, because when he spoke, it was with a voice I knew. Muffled by the mask enough that I couldn't place it, but I knew it, all right.

"Joey?"

I tried to say "Yeah?" but all I could manage was some kind of noise in my throat.

He took a step toward me. "Look, this is all happening a

bit fast for you, I imagine, but you have to trust me."

All happening a bit fast? Understatement of the decade, dude, I wanted to tell him. My house wasn't my house, my family wasn't my family, my girlfriend wasn't my girlfriend—well, she hadn't been from the start, but this was no time to get finicky. The point was that everything stable and permanent in my life had turned to Jell-O, and I was about *this* far from losing it completely.

Then the weirdo in the Halloween mask put his hand on my shoulder, and that closed the gap between losing and lost. I didn't care if he was someone I knew. I jerked my knee up, hard, just as Mr. Dimas had told us all to do—boys *and* girls—if we ever thought we were in physical danger from a male adult. ("Don't aim *for* the testicles," said Mr. Dimas that day, just as if he were discussing the weather. "Aim for the center of his stomach, as if you're planning to get there *through* the testicles. Then don't stop to see if he's okay or not. Just run.")

I practically broke my kneecap. He was wearing some kind of armor under the coat.

I yelped in pain and clutched my right knee. What made it worse was that I knew that behind mirrored mask, the creep was smiling.

"You okay?" he asked in that half-familiar voice. He sounded more amused than concerned.

"You mean apart from not knowing what's going on, losing my family and breaking my knee?" I would have run, but fleeing for one's life requires two legs in good operating condition. I took a deep breath, tried to pull it together.

"Two of those things are your own stupid fault. I was hoping to get to you before you started Walking, but I wasn't fast enough. Now you've set off every alarm in this region by crossing from plane to plane like that."

I had no idea what he was talking about; I hadn't been on a plane since the family saw Aunt Agatha for Easter. I rubbed my leg.

"Who are you?" I said. "Take off the mask."

He didn't. "You can call me Jay," he said. Or maybe it was, "You can call me J." He put out his hand again, as if I were meant to shake it.

I wonder if I would have shaken it or not—I never got to find out. A sudden flash of green light left me blinded and blinking, and, a moment later, a loud bang momentarily put my ears out of commission, too.

"Run!" shouted Jay. "No, not that way! Go the way you came. I'll try to head them off."

I didn't run—I just stood there, staring.

There were three flying disks, silver and glittering, hovering in the air about ten feet away. Riding each disk, balancing like a surfer riding a wave, was a man wearing a gray one-piece outfit. Each of the men was holding what looked like a weighted net—like something a fisherman might have, it occurred to me, or a gladiator.

"Joseph Harker," called one of the gladiators in a flat, almost expressionless voice. "Opposition is nonproductive. Please remain where you are." He waved his net to emphasize his point.

The net crackled and sparked tiny blue sparks where the mesh touched. I knew two things when I saw those nets: that they were for me, and that they were going to hurt if they caught me.

Jay shoved me. *"Run!"*

This time, I got it. I turned and took off.

One of the men on the disks shouted in pain. I looked back momentarily: He was tumbling down to the ground while the disk hovered in the air above him. I suspected that Jay was responsible.

The other two gladiators were hanging in the air directly above me, keeping pace with me as I ran. I didn't have to look up. I could see their shadows.

I felt like a wild beast—a lion or a tiger, maybe—on a wildlife documentary, being hunted by men with tranquilizer darts. You know that it's going to be brought down, if it just keeps running in a straight line. So I didn't. I dodged to the left, just as a net landed where I had been. It brushed my right hand as it fell: My hand felt numb and I could not feel my fingers.

And I *moved.*

I was not sure how I did it, or even what I had just done. I had a momentary impression of more fog and twinkling lights and the sounds of wind chimes, and then I was alone. The men in the sky were gone—even mysterious Mr. Jay with the mirror face was nowhere to be seen. It was a quiet October afternoon, wet leaves were sticking to the sidewalk and nothing was happening in sleepy Greenville as per usual.

My heart was thumping so hard I thought my chest was going to burst.

I walked down Maple Road, trying to catch my breath, rubbing my numb right hand with my left, trying to get a handle on what had just happened.

My house wasn't my house any longer. The people who lived there weren't my family. There were bad guys on flying manhole covers after me, and a guy with an armored crotch and a mirrored face.

What could I do? Go to the police? *Suuure*, I told myself. They hear stories like this one all the time. They send the people who tell them stories like that to the funny farm.

That left one person I could talk to. I came around the curve in the street and saw Greenville High in front of me.

I was going to talk to Mr. Dimas.

CHAPTER FOUR

Greenville High School was built nearly fifty years ago. The city closed it when I was a kid for a few months to remove the asbestos. There are a couple of temporary trailers out in the back that house the art rooms and the science labs, and will do until they get around to building the new extension. It's kind of crumbling; it smells like damp and pizza and sweaty sports equipment—and if I don't sound like I love my school, well, I guess that's because I don't. But I had to admit it made me feel pretty good to be there now.

I made it up the steps, keeping a wary eye on the sky for gladiators on flying disks. Nothing.

I walked inside. Nobody gave me a second glance.

It was the middle of fifth period, and there weren't too many people in the halls. I headed for Dimas's classroom as fast as I could without running. He'd never been my favorite teacher—those bizarre tests he came up with were hard—but he'd always impressed me as someone who wouldn't lose his head in an emergency.

If this wasn't an emergency, I didn't know what was. And it was his fault, in a way, wasn't it?

I didn't quite run down the corridor until I got to his classroom. I looked through the glass of the door. He was sitting at his desk, marking a stack of homework papers. I knocked on the door. He didn't look up, just said "Come!" and kept on marking.

I opened the door and went over to his desk. He kept his eyes on the papers.

"Mr. Dimas?" I tried to keep my voice from shaking. "Do you have a moment?"

He looked up, looked into my eyes, and he dropped his pen. Just dropped it, like that. I bent down, picked it up and put it back on his desk.

I said, "Is there something wrong?"

He looked pale and—it took me a few moments to recognize this—actually frightened. His jaw dropped. He shook his head in the way my dad always called "shaking out the cobwebs" and looked at me again. He held out his right hand.

Then he said, "Shake my hand."

"Uh, Mr. Dimas . . . ?" I was suddenly seized by the fear that he was part of all this weirdness, too, and the thought frightened me so that I could barely keep standing. I needed someone to be the adult right now.

He still held his hand out. His fingers were shaking, I noticed. "You look like you've seen a ghost," I told him.

He looked at me sharply. "That's not funny, Joey. If you

are Joey. Shake my hand."

I put my hand in his. He squeezed it just short of painfully, feeling the flesh and the bones of it, then he let go and looked up at me. "You're real," he said. "You aren't a hallucination. What does this mean? *Are* you Joey Harker? You certainly look like him."

"Of course I'm Joey," I said. I'll admit it—I was ready to start bawling like a baby. This madness, whatever it was, couldn't be affecting him as well. Mr. Dimas was always so sane. Well, kind of sane. When Mayor Haenkle described him in his column in the *Greenville Courier* as "crazy as a snowblower in June" I pretty much knew what he meant.

But I had to tell someone what was going on, and Mr. Dimas still seemed like the best choice.

"Look," I said carefully, "today has gone . . . really weird. You're the only person I thought could maybe handle it."

He was still as pale as a pitcher of milk, but he nodded. Then there was a knock on the door and he said, "Come!" He sounded relieved.

It was Ted Russell. He hardly even glanced at me. "Mr. Dimas," he said. "I got a problem. If I get an F in Social Studies it means I don't get a car. And I figure you're going to give me an F."

Apparently some things even alternate realities couldn't change; Ted was obviously still grade challenged. Mr. Dimas had looked disappointed when Ted came in; now he was annoyed. "And why exactly is this my problem, Edward?"

That was the Mr. Dimas I remembered. I felt relieved, and before I could think the better of it, I had already spoken. "He's right, Ted. Anyway, keeping you off the road is a public service. You're a five-car pileup waiting to happen."

He turned on me, and I hoped that he wasn't going to hit me in front of Mr. Dimas. Ted Russell likes to hit people smaller than him, and that takes in a big chunk of the school population. He raised a hand—then he saw it was me.

He stopped, hand in the air, and said, plain as day, "Mother of God, it's a judgment on me," and started to cry. Then he ran out of the room. He ran like I had run earlier. *It's called running for your life*, I thought.

I looked at Mr. Dimas. He looked back, then hooked one foot around a nearby chair leg and dragged the chair toward me. "Sit," he told me. "Put your head down. Breathe slow."

I did. Good thing, too, because the world—or at least his office—had gone kind of wobbly. After a minute things steadied, and I raised my head. Mr. Dimas was watching me.

He walked out of the room, returned a few seconds later with a paper cup. "Drink."

I drank the water. It helped. A little.

"I thought I was having a weird day before. Now it's somewhere out beyond bizarre. Can you explain any of this to me?"

He nodded. "I can explain a little of it, certainly. At least,

I can explain Edward's reaction. And mine. You see, Joey Harker drowned last year in an accident down at Grand River Falls."

I grabbed my sanity and held on with both hands. "I didn't drown," I told him. "I got pretty shaken up, and I had to have four stitches in my leg, and Dad said that would teach me a lesson I'd never forget, and that trying to go over the falls in a barrel was the single stupidest thing I'd ever tried, and I told him I wouldn't have done it if Ted hadn't said I was chicken. . . ."

"You drowned," said Mr. Dimas flatly. "I helped pull your body out of the river. I spoke at your memorial service."

"Oh . . ." We both were quiet then for a moment, until the quiet got to be too much and I had to say something. So I said, "What did you say?" Well, wouldn't you have asked the same thing, if you were me?

"Nice things," he said. "I told them you were a good-hearted kid, and I told them how you got lost all the time in your first semester here. How we'd have to send out search parties to get you safely to Phys. Ed. or the science trailers."

My cheeks were burning. "Great," I said with all the sarcasm I could muster. "That's just how I'd want to be remembered."

"Joey," he asked gently, "what are you doing here?"

"Having a weird day—I told you." And I was going to explain it all to him—and I bet he would have figured out some of it—but before I could say anything else, the room began to go dark. Not dark as in, the sun went behind a cloud dark, or dark as in, hey, that's a mighty scary thunderstorm dark, or even dark as in, I'll bet this is what a total eclipse of the sun looks like. This was dark like something you could *touch*, something solid and tangible and cold.

And there were eyes in the middle of the darkness.

The darkness formed itself into a shape. It was a woman. Her hair was long and black. She had big lips, like it had been fashionable for movie stars to have back when I was a kid; she was small and kind of thin, and her eyes were so green she had to have been wearing contacts, except she wasn't.

They looked like a cat's eyes. I don't mean they were shaped like cat's eyes. I mean they looked at me the way a cat looks at a bird.

"Joseph Harker," she said.

"Yes," I said. Which was probably not the smartest thing I could've said, because then she laid a spell on me.

That's the best way I can explain it. She moved her finger in the air so that it traced a figure—a symbol that looked a little bit Chinese and a little bit Egyptian—that hung glowing in the air after her finger finished moving, and she said something at the same time; and the word she said hung and vibrated and swam through the room; and the whole of it, word and gesture, filled my head; and I knew I had to follow her for all my life, wherever she went. I would follow her or die in the attempt.

The door opened. Two men came in. One was wearing just a rag, like a diaper around his middle. He was bald—in fact, as near as I could tell, he was completely hairless, and that, with the diaper, made him look like a bad dream even without the tattoos. The tats just made it worse: They covered every inch of his skin from hairline to toenails; he was all faded blues and greens and reds and blacks, picture after picture. I couldn't see what they were, even though he wasn't more than five feet away.

The other man was wearing a T-shirt and jeans. The T-shirt was a size too small, which was really too bad, because it left a big stretch of stomach exposed. And his stomach . . . well, it *glistened*. Like a jellyfish. I could see bones and nerves and things through his jelly skin. I looked at his face, and it was the same way. His skin was like an oil slick over his bones, muscles and tendons; you could see them, wavery and distorted, beneath it.

The woman looked at them as if she'd been expecting them. She gestured casually at me. "Got him," she said. "Like taking ambrosia from an elemental. Easy. He'll follow us anywhere now."

Mr. Dimas stood up and said, "Now, listen here, young lady. You people can't—" and then she made another gesture and he froze. Or kind of. I could see his muscles trembling, as if he were trying to move, trying with every cell of his being, and still failing.

"Where's the pickup?" she asked. She had a kind of Valley Girl accent, which I found irritating, particularly since I knew I was going to have to spend the rest of my life following her around.

"Outside. There's a blasted oak," said the jellyfish man in a voice like belching mud. "They'll take us from there."

"Good," she said. Then she looked at me. "Come along," she told me in a voice that sounded like she was talking to a dog she didn't particularly like. She turned and walked away.

Blindly, obediently, I followed her, hating myself with every step.

INTERLOG

From Jay's Journal

I'd got back to Base Town late at night. Most of the folk in my dorm were asleep, except Jai, and he was meditating, suspended in midair with his legs crossed, so he might as well have been sleeping. I crept around, undressed and showered for twenty minutes, getting the mud and dried blood out of my hair. Then I filled out the damage & loss report, explaining how I'd lost my jacket and belt (I traded the jacket for information, and the belt had made a pretty effective tourniquet, if you must know). Then I crashed like a dead man and slept till I woke.

It's a tradition. You don't wake a guy when he gets back from a job. He gets a day to debrief, and then a day to himself. It's kind of sacrosanct. But sacrosanct goes out the window when the Old Man calls, and there was a note beside my bunk when I awoke, on the Old Man's orange paper, telling me to report to his office at my convenience, which is his way of saying immediately.

I pulled on my gear and I headed for the commander's office.

There are five hundred of us on the base, and every single one of us would die for the Old Man. Not that he'd want us to. He needs us. We need us.

I knew he was in a foul mood when I reached the anteroom. His assistant waved me into his office as soon as she saw me coming. No "hello," not even an offer of coffee. Just "He's waiting. Go on in."

The Old Man's desk takes up most of the room, and it's covered with piles of paper and dog-eared folders held together with rubber bands. Heaven only knows how he finds anything on there.

On the wall behind him there's a huge picture of something that looks kind of like a whirlpool and kind of like a tornado and mostly like the shape the water makes as it goes down the drain. It's an image of the Altiverse—the pattern that we all swore to protect and to guard and, if needed, to give our lives for.

He glared at me with his good eye. "Sit down, Jay."

The Old Man looks to be in his fifties, but he could be much older than that. He's pretty banged up. One of his eyes is artificial: it's a Binary construct, made of metal and glass. Lights flicker inside it, green and violet and blue. When he looks at you through it, it can have you checking out your conscience and make you feel five years old every bit as well as his real eye can. His real eye is brown, just like mine.

"You're late," he growled.

"Yes, sir," I said. "I came as soon as I got your message."

"We have a new Walker," he told me. He picked up a file from his desk, riffled through it and pulled out a sheet of blue paper. He passed it to me. "Upstairs thinks he could be hot."

"How hot?"

"Not sure. But he's a wild card. Going to be setting off alarms and tripping snares everywhere he goes."

35

I looked at the paper. Basic human-friendly planet design—one of the middle worlds, the thick part of the Arc—nothing too exotic. The coordinates were pretty straightforward as well. It looked like a fairly easy run.

"Reel him in?"

The Old Man nodded. "Yeah. And quickly. They'll both be sending out grab teams to get him as soon as they know he's out there."

"I'm meant to be debriefing the Starlight job today."

"Joliet and Joy are debriefing now. If I need any amplification I can get in touch with you. This takes priority. And you can have two days off when it's done."

I wondered if I'd actually get the two days off. It didn't matter. "Got it. I'll bring him in."

"Dismissed," said the Old Man. I stood up, figuring on a quick trip to the armory and then out into the field and into the In-Between. Before I reached the door, though, he spoke again. He was still growling at me, but it was a friendly growl. "Remember, Jay, I need you back here in one piece, and I need you back here soon. One more Walker, more or less, isn't going to mean the end of the worlds. One less field officer might. Stay out of trouble. You'll be back and debriefing by oh seven hundred hours tomorrow."

"Yes, sir," I said, and closed the door.

The Old Man's assistant handed me my armory requisition slip. Then she smiled at me. Her name's Josetta. "Goes for me, too,

Jay," she said. "Come back safe. We need all the field ops we can get."

The quartermaster is from one of the heavier Earths—places where you feel like you weigh five hundred pounds, and often do. He's shaped like a barrel, ten inches taller than I am. Looking at him is like looking into a distorting mirror at a carnival, the kind that squashes you as it magnifies you.

I requisitioned an encounter suit, watched him toss it down to me like it didn't weigh anything at all. I caught it, and it almost knocked me over. It must have weighed seventy-five pounds. I figured he was mad at me for losing the combat jacket and the belt.

I signed for the encounter suit. I stripped down to my T-shirt and boxers, draped it over me and activated it, feeling it cover my body from head to toe; and then I set my mind on the new kid. I got a bead on him and began to Walk toward him. . . .

The In-Between was cold, and it tasted like vanilla and woodsmoke in my mouth. I found him without a hitch. And then it all went wrong.

CHAPTER FIVE

I was walking after the witch, with Mr. Jellyfish and the tattooed man just behind me.

It was like two people were living in my head. One of them was ME, a big huge me, who had somehow decided that the most important thing there ever was or would be was the witch woman he was following out of the high school. The other person in my head was me, too, but a tiny little me who was screaming silently, who was terrified of the witch and the tattooed man and Mr. Jellyfish, who wanted to run, to save himself.

Trouble was, the little me was having no effect whatsoever. We crossed the football field, heading toward the old oak tree, which had been struck by lightning a couple of years back and now just stuck up into the sky like a rotten tooth. The sun had just gone down, but the sky was still light. I was shivering.

The witch turned to the tattooed man. "Scarabus, contact the transport."

He bowed his head. I could see goose bumps on his skin under one of those not-quite-clear images. He raised a finger and touched it to one of the tattoos on his neck, and suddenly I could see that one clearly. It was a ship under sail. He closed his eyes. When he opened them, the pupils were glowing gently.

"The ship *Lacrimae Mundi* at your bidding, lady," he said in a distant voice like a radio broadcast.

"I have our quarry safely here. Bring her in, captain."

"As you wish," said the tattooed man, in the distant voice. Then he closed his eyes and took his hand off his tattoo; and when he opened his eyes, they were normal once more. "What's the word?" he asked in his normal voice.

"They're bringing her in now," said the jellyfish man. "Look!"

I raised my head.

The ship—it seemed as big as the auditorium—that was materializing in the air in front of us looked like every pirate ship you've ever seen in old movies: stained wooden planks, big billowing sails, and a figurehead of a man with the head of a shark. It was gliding toward us about five feet above the ground, and the green grass of the football field tossed back and forth like the surface of the sea as it passed.

The big me couldn't have cared less about ghost ships sailing through the air, as long as the witch lady and I were together. The little me that was trapped in the back of my head was sort of hoping that all this was just a bad reaction to some new medication the nice doctors were trying on me in whatever mental hospital they had me locked up in.

A rope ladder was thrown over the side of the ship.

"Climb!" said the witch woman, and I climbed.

When I was up over the side of the ship, huge hands grabbed me and dropped me on the deck like a sack of potatoes. I looked up to see men the size of wrestlers dressed like sailors in pirate movies. They had scarves tied around their heads and worn old sweaters and battered jeans, and were barefoot. They were more careful with the witch woman, lifting her carefully over the side of the ship. They all backed away then. I guessed that they didn't want to touch the jellyfish man or Scarabus, the tattooed guy, and I couldn't really blame them.

One of the sailors looked down at me. "Is *that* what all the fuss is about?" he asked. "That shrimp?"

"Yes," said the witch woman coldly. "That shrimp is what all the fuss is about."

"Lumme," said the sailor. "Are we going to drop him overboard, then? Once we're under way?"

"Hurt him before we get back to HEX and every warlock in the Tarn will want a little piece of your hide," she told him. "He dies *our* way. What do you think powers this ship of yours, anyway? Take him down to my quarters."

She turned to me. "Joseph, you need to go with this man. Stay where he tells you to stay. To do otherwise would make me very unhappy."

The idea of hurting her made my heart ache. Literally—there was a stabbing pain inside me. I knew that I could never do anything to make her unhappy in any way. I would wait for her until the world ended if I had to.

The sailor showed me down a flight of steps into a narrow corridor that smelled like floor polish and fish. At the end of the corridor there was a door, and we opened it.

"Here we are, my fine shrimp," he said. "The Lady Indigo's quarters for the voyage back to HEX. You stand here and wait for her. If you need to relieve yourself, there's a lavatory back there, through that door. Use it; don't befoul yourself. She'll be down when she's ready. Got to chart our course back now, she does, with the captain."

He was talking to me like you'd talk to a pet or a farm animal, just to hear the sound of his own voice.

He went out.

There was a lurching, then, and through the round cabin window I could see the evening sky dissolve into stars, thousands of them, floating in a violet blackness. We were moving.

I must have stood there for hours, waiting beside the door.

At one point I realized I needed to pee, and I went through the door that the sailor had pointed to. I suppose I expected something cramped and old-fashioned, but what waited behind the door was a small but luxurious bathroom with a large pink bathtub and a small pink-marble toilet. Which I used and flushed. I washed my hands with pink soap that smelled like roses and dried my hands on a fluffy pink bath towel.

Then I looked out the bathroom porthole.

Above the ship were stars. Below the ship the stars continued, shimmering points of light. There were more stars than I had ever imagined existed. And they were different. I didn't recognize any of the constellations Dad had taught me when I was young. A lot of them were impossibly close— close enough to show disks as big as the sun, but somehow it was still night.

I wondered when we would get where we were going.

I wondered why they were going to have to kill me when we got there (and somewhere inside me a tiny Joey Harker screamed and yelled and sobbed and tried to get my body's attention).

I hoped that the Lady Indigo hadn't returned to find that I wasn't waiting for her. The idea of disappointing her ripped through me like a knife in the heart, and I ran back to the doorway and stood at attention, hoping she would come back soon. If she didn't come back, I was certain I would die.

I waited another twenty minutes or so, and then the door opened and happiness, pure and undiluted, flooded my soul. My Lady Indigo was here, with Scarabus.

She did not spare me a glance. She sat on the small pink

bed, while the tattooed man stood in front of her.

"I don't know," she said to him, apparently responding to a question he had posed to her in the corridor. "I cannot imagine that anyone could find us here. And as soon as we reach HEX, there are guards and wards such as there are nowhere else in the Altiverse."

"Still," he said sulkily, "Neville said he picked up a disturbance in the continuum. He said something was coming."

"Neville," she said sweetly, "is a jelly-fleshed worrywart. The *Lacrimae Mundi* is sailing back to HEX through the Nowhere-at-All. We're practically undetectable."

"Practically," he muttered.

She stood up and walked over to me. "How are you, Joseph Harker?"

"Very happy to see you back here, my lady," I told her.

"Did anything unusual happen while you were down here waiting for me?"

"Unusual? I don't think so."

"Thank you, Joseph. You need not speak until next I tell you to." She pursed her big lips and went back to sit on the bed again. "Scarabus, contact HEX for me."

"Yes, my lady."

He touched a tattoo on his stomach, a tattoo that looked a bit like something from the Arabian Nights, a bit like Dracula's castle and a bit like the world seen from space. He closed his eyes. When he opened them again, his pupils were flickering with light—not glowing steadily, as they had when he had summoned the ship to the football field.

He spoke in a deep sort of voice then, the sort of voice you'd get if you dipped Darth Vader in a giant vat of maple syrup.

"Indigo? What is it?"

"We have the boy Harker, my lord Dogknife. A world-class Walker: He will power many ships."

"Good," said the syrupy wheeze. Even under whatever spell I was under, that voice made my skin crawl. "We are ready to begin the assault on the Lorimare worlds. The phantom gateways we will be creating will make a counter-attack or rescue impossible. When they are empowered, the usual Lorimare coordinates will then open notional shadow realms under our control. Now, with another fine Harker at our disposal, we will have all the power we need to send in the fleet. The Imperator of the Lorimare worlds is already one of ours."

"We have the Cause, Lord Dogknife."

"We have the Will, Lady Indigo. How long until you dock here?"

"Twelve hours, no less."

"Very well. I shall prepare a vat for the Harker."

She looked at me and smiled, and my heart leapt up within me and sang like a cardinal in springtime.

"I would like to keep a souvenir of this Harker," she said.

44

"Perhaps a hank of his hair or a knucklebone."

"I shall give orders to that effect. Now, good day," and the tattooed man closed his eyes. When he opened them, he said in his own voice, "Ow. That left me with a killer headache. How was Dogknife?"

"Excellent," she said. "He is planning our assault on the Lorimare worlds."

"Better him than me," said Scarabus, and he rubbed his temple. "Ow. I could do with a walk up on deck. Breath of fresh air."

She nodded. "Yes. I've spent the last couple of hours down in the map room, breathing the captain's meal of raw onions and goat cheese." She looked at me. "But I don't want to leave the Harker here."

Scarabus shrugged his thin blue-and-red shoulders. "Bring him with."

She nodded. "Very well," she said. "One moment." She went through the door to the little pink bathroom and closed the door behind her.

The tattooed man looked at me. "You sad little creature," he said. "Like a lamb to the slaughter."

The Lady Indigo had not told me to speak, so I said nothing.

There was a tapping on the cabin door. Scarabus opened it. I couldn't see what happened next, because the door blocked my view. But there was a thud, and a gasp, and

Scarabus collapsed to the floor. The man who came in was wearing a hat and a coat and a silver face.

He raised a hand to greet me. Then he stripped off his raincoat and his hat. He was covered from head to foot in a silver suit of some kind, like a man wearing a mirror. He rolled the unconscious Scarabus behind the bed and put the coat over him.

I could hear the sink running. I knew that my Lady Indigo was washing her hands with the pink rose-smelling soap. I had to warn her that the Jay man was there and that he meant her harm. I tried to speak, but she hadn't given me permission to talk, and so the words would not come.

Jay—if that was who the man in the mirror suit was—raised a hand to the suit and adjusted something above his heart.

The suit flowed and changed and . . .

Scarabus standing there in front of me. If I hadn't been able to see the real tattooed man's foot peeping out from under the coat on the other side of the bed, I would have thought Jay really was him. The illusion was that good.

My Lady Indigo came out of the bathroom.

Tell me to speak, I thought, pleading with her, *tell me to speak, and I will tell you you're in danger. This is not your friend. I am the only person who truly cares about you, and I cannot warn you.*

"Right," she said. "Let's go up on deck. How's your headache?"

The man who looked like Scarabus shrugged. I guessed that the suit didn't work for voices. Lady Indigo didn't press the point. She turned and went out of the room. "Follow me, slave Harker, and stay close," she called.

I followed her up onto the deck. I couldn't even begin to imagine not doing so. (The Joey buried deep inside me could—he kept on yelling and screaming that I should resist, run, *anything*. I kept walking. His words meant nothing.)

Above us star fields spun and blinked and whorled. Neville the jelly man hurried over as soon as he spotted us.

"I've checked all the instruments and portents," he said self-importantly, in his sucking-mud voice, "and consulted the astrolabe, and they are all quite certain. We are carrying a stowaway. Some presence arrived on the *Lacrimae Mundi* about an hour ago. Just when I said I felt something in the pit of my stomach."

"And a mighty stomach it is, too," said the mirror man pretending to be Scarabus in Scarabus's voice. I was wrong, then; the suit could do voices, too.

"I shall ignore that comment," said the jelly man to Scarabus.

"What kind of stowaway, Neville?" asked Lady Indigo.

"Could be one of Graceful Zelda's people trying to grab the Harker, so they can take all the credit," said Scarabus. "You know how much she hates you. If she took your Harker

47

back to HEX, it would make her look very good."

"Zelda." Lady Indigo made a face, as if she'd bitten into something that had turned out to be mostly maggots.

Neville hugged himself with his jellyfish hands and looked miserable. "She wants my skin," he said. "Has for years. Wants a coat, Zelda does, one that'll let her show off and still be warm."

Before he could continue, Scarabus—Jay pretending to be Scarabus—looked at me and squinted. "My lady," he said, "how do you know this is still your Harker? What if it's some kind of changeling? They could have already stolen the boy away and left something behind that only looks like him. Some kind of spell creature, perhaps. Easy enough to do, even here."

Lady Indigo frowned and looked at me. Then she gestured in the air with one hand while she sang three clear notes. "Now," she said, "any spell that is on or around you is removed. Let us see what you truly are."

I realized that I could speak again if I wanted to.

I could do anything I wanted to now.

I was back in charge, and, boy, did it feel good to be back.

"Right, Joey," said the Scarabus imposter, his face and body flowing back into silver.

"Jay? Is that you?"

"Of course it's me! Come on!" He picked me up in a fireman's carry and ran.

We made it almost to the rail when there was a small green explosion, like a firecracker going off, and Jay made a noise of pain. I shifted my head, stared at his opposite shoulder. The mirror stuff covering it was seared and gone, exposing a mass of circuitry and skin, and most of the skin was bleeding. I could see the bizarre, distorted images of Lady Indigo, Neville and Scarabus reflected from his back.

He dropped me.

We were up against the edge of the ship. On the other side of the bulwark was . . . nothing. Just stars and moons and galaxies, going on forever.

Lady Indigo raised her hand. A small bead of green fire hung in her palm.

Neville had a huge, nasty-looking sword in one hand. I don't know where it came from, but it glistened and jiggled just like his skin. He started walking toward us.

I heard something above us and looked up. The rigging was filled with sailors, and the sailors all had knives.

Things were definitely not looking good.

I heard a clattering on the deck. "Don't shoot them, my lady! Hold your fire!" The real Scarabus stumbled up from below.

He seemed like an unlikely saviour.

"Please," he said. "Let me. This calls for something special." He extended one tattoo-covered arm at us and moved his other hand toward his bicep. There was a blurry image of a huge serpent curled around his upper arm. I was pretty sure that if he touched that tattoo, the snake would be real, and big—and undoubtedly hungry.

There was only one thing left to do, so we did it.

We jumped.

INTERLOG 2

From Jay's Journal

Looking back on it, I made a couple of seriously wrong calls. The wrongest was deciding to meet the new kid outside his parents' house in the new world that he'd slipped into.

I was hoping that he wouldn't start Walking before I got to him. But hope pays no dividends, as the Old Man says. ("Hope when you've got nothing else," he once told us. "But if you've got anything else, then for Heaven's sake, DO it!") And Joey had already started Walking.

Not far. He'd done what most new Walkers do—slipped into a world he wasn't in. It's harder to Walk into a world in which "you" exist already: It's like identical magnetic poles repelling. He needed an out, and so he slipped into a world in which he wasn't.

Which meant that it took me an extra forty minutes to locate him, Walking from plane to plane. Finally I tracked him—he was on a crosstown bus, headed home. Or what he thought was home.

And I waited outside his home. I suppose I figured that he'd be more amenable to reason once he saw what was waiting for him in there.

But, as the Old Man pointed out that morning, he must have tripped every alarm in creation when he started Walking.

And he was in no state to be talked to when he came out of that house. Which meant we were sitting ducks for the Binary retiarii on their Gravitrons, waving their nets around.

Given the alternatives, I don't know which I hate worse: the Binary or the HEX folk.

HEX boils young Walkers down to their essences. I mean that literally—they put us in huge pots, like in those cannibal cartoons you used to see in the back of newspapers, and surround it with a web of spells and wards. Then they boil us down to nothing but our essence—our souls, if you will—which they force into glass pots. And they use those glass pots to power their ships and any multi-world traveling they do.

The Binary treat Walkers differently, but no better. They chill us to negative 273°, a hair above absolute zero, hang us from meat hooks, then seal us in these huge hangars on their homeworld, with pipes and wires going into the back of our heads, and keep us there, not quite dead but a long, long way from alive, while they drain our energy and use it to power their interplane travel.

If it's possible to hate two organizations exactly the same, then that's how much I hate them.

So Joey did the smart thing—unconsciously, but it was still smart—when the Binary goons showed up. He Walked between worlds again.

I took out the three retiarii without any trouble.

Then I had to find him again. And if I'd thought it hard the first time . . . well, this time he'd charged blindly through the

Altiverse, ripping his way through hundreds of probability layers as if they were tissue paper. Like a bull going through a china shop—or a couple of thousand identical china shops.

So I started after him. Again.

It's strange. I'd forgotten how much I hated these newer Greenvilles. The Greenville I grew up in still had drive-in burger bars with waitresses on roller skates, black-and-white TV and the Green Hornet on the radio. These Greenvilles had mini satellite dishes on the roofs of the houses and people driving cars that looked like giant eggs or like jeeps on steroids. No fins among the lot of them. They had color TVs and video games and home theaters and the Internet. What they didn't have any more was a town. And they hadn't even noticed its passing.

I hit a fairly distant Greenville, and finally I felt him like a flare in my mind. I Walked toward him. And saw a HEX ship, all billowing sails and hokey rigging, fading out into the Nowhere-at-All.

I'd lost him. Again. Probably for good this time.

I sat down on the football field and thought hard.

I had two options. One was easy. One was going to be a son of a bitch.

I could go back and tell the Old Man that I'd failed. That HEX had captured a Joseph Harker who had more worldwalking power than any ten Walkers put together. That it wasn't my fault. And we'd let the matter drop there. Maybe he'd chew me out, maybe he wouldn't, but I knew that he knew that I'd rake myself over the coals for this one harder and longer than he ever could. Easy.

Or I could try the impossible. It's a long way back to HEX in one of those galleons. I could try to find Joey Harker and his captors in the Nowhere-at-All. It's the kind of thing we joke about, back at base. No one's ever done it. No one ever could.

I couldn't face telling the Old Man I'd screwed up. It was easier to try the impossible.

So I did.

I Walked into the Nowhere-at-All. And I discovered something none of us knew: Those ships leave a wake. It's almost a pattern, or a disturbance, in the star fields they fly through. It's very faint, and only a Walker could sense it.

I had to let the Old Man know about this. This was important. I wondered if the Binary saucers left trails you could follow through the Static.

The only thing we at InterWorld have going for us is this: We can get there long before they can. What takes them hours or days or weeks of travel through the Static or through the Nowhere-at-All, we can do in seconds or minutes, via the In-Between.

I blessed the encounter suit, which minimized the windburn and the cold. Not to mention protected me from the retiarii nets.

I could see the ship in the distance, HEX flags fluttering in the nothingness. I could feel Joey burning like a beacon in my mind. Poor kid. I wondered if he knew what was in store for him if I failed.

I landed on the ship from below and behind, holding on between the rudder and the side of the stern. I waited for a while. They'd have at least a couple of world-class magicians on the ship, and, though the encounter suit would mask me to some extent, it wouldn't hide the fact that something had changed. I gave them time enough to hunt through the ship and find nothing. Then I went in through a porthole and followed the trail to where they were keeping the kid.

I'm recording this in the In-Between on the way back to base. It'll make debriefing quicker and easier tomorrow.

Memo to the Old Man: I want both days off when this is done. I deserve them.

CHAPTER SIX

Well, to be 100 percent truthful about it, "we" didn't really jump. Jay jumped, and he was holding onto my windbreaker, so I didn't really have a lot of choice. My exit was more in the tradition of the Three Stooges than Errol Flynn. I probably would have broken my neck when we landed.

Except we didn't land.

There was no place *to* land. We just kept falling. I looked down and could glimpse stars shining through the thin mists below us. A green firecracker explosion happened off to the left of us, buffeting us and knocking us to the right, but it was too far away to do any damage. Above us, the ship swiftly shrank to the size of a bottle cap and then vanished in the darkness above. And Jay and I hurtled into the darkness below.

You know how skydivers rhapsodize about free fall being like flying? I realized then that they had to be lying. It feels like falling. The wind screams past your ears, rushes into your mouth and up your nose, and you have no doubt whatsoever that you're falling to your death. There's a reason it's called "terminal velocity."

This wasn't a parachute jump, and we weren't near Earth or any other planet I could see, but we were definitely falling down, down, down. We must have fallen a good five minutes when Jay finally grabbed my shoulders and wrestled me around so that my ear was next to his mouth. He shouted something, but even with his lips only an inch or so from my ear I couldn't understand him.

"What?" I screamed back.

He pulled me closer still and shouted, *"There's a portal below us! Walk!"*

The first and last time I'd tried to walk on air I was five—I'd strolled blithely off the edge of a six-foot-high cinderblock wall and gotten a broken collarbone for my efforts. They say a cat that walks on a hot stove will never walk on a cold one, and I guess there's some truth in that—certainly I never again tried to grow wings.

Until now. Now I didn't really have a choice.

Jay obviously could tell what I was thinking. "Walk, brother, or we'll fall through the Nowhere-at-All until the wind strips the flesh from our bones! *Walk!* Not with your legs—with your *mind!*"

I had no more idea of how to do what he was telling me than a bullfrog knows how to croak the *Nutcracker Suite*. But he was surely right about one thing—there didn't seem to be any other way out of our predicament. So I took a deep breath and tried to focus my mind.

It didn't help that I had no idea what I was trying to focus on. "Walk!" Jay had commanded me. But in order to walk I needed something solid to walk *on*. So that's what I concentrated on—my feet treading solid ground.

At first nothing changed. Then I noticed that the screaming wind hitting us from below was lessening. At the same time the mist was thickening. I couldn't see the stars beneath us anymore. And there was a strange luminescence that seemed to come from the mist that now surrounded us.

We were floating more than falling now. It was like falling in a dream, and it came as no surprise to either of us when we touched down on what seemed to be a cloud.

I suppose Jay had done stranger stuff than this before, and that was why he took it in stride, so to speak. As for me, I had just reached a saturation point, that was all. Considering what I'd been through today, I'd finally come to the conclusion that this was probably all going on between my ears, that I'd somehow fried my brain's motherboard and that I was probably at that moment wearing a wraparound canvas jacket with padlocks for buttons. Most likely they had me up in the sanitarium at Rook's Bay, sitting in a very soft room and eating very soft food. A pretty depressing prospect, but it did have an upside—nothing could surprise me anymore.

Which thought gave me a little comfort for about two more minutes—and then the mists thinned out completely, and I saw where we were.

I'd gotten a glimpse of this—place? condition? state of mind?—back when Jay had come through that slit in the air to meet me. This was the same, only this time he and I were in the middle of it.

"Well done, Joey," said Jay. "You got us here. You did it."

I stared, turning slowly. There was a *lot* to see.

We were no longer on a cloud. I stood on a purple pathway that snaked, apparently unsupported, off into . . . infinity. There was no horizon—wherever we were did not seem to have any boundaries—but there was no skyline either. The distance was simply lost in more distance. Jay stood next to me on a magenta strip that wound off in the same general direction; it sometimes passed under, sometimes over my path. The colors were vivid, and both paths had the sheen of dyed polyurethane.

But that wasn't all. Not by several decimal places.

On eye level with me and about three feet away was a geometric shape, larger than my head, that pulsed and throbbed, presenting now five sides, now nine, now sixteen. I couldn't have told you what it was made of any more than I could tell you why it was doing what it was doing. I suppose you could say it was made out of *yellow*, because that's the color it was saturated with. I touched it, gingerly, with one finger. It had the texture of linoleum.

I looked in another direction—and just had time to duck as a spinning *something* whizzed by me, skittering erratically as it dodged and weaved through the chaos around it. A moment later it splashed into a pool of what looked like mercury—except that it was the color of cinnamon, and the pool hung at a forty-five-degree angle to the strip I stood on. The waves and droplets of the splash slowed as they spread, ultimately freezing at the height of the splatter.

This sort of stuff was going on all around us, nonstop. What looked like a stylized mouth opened up in midair not far from Jay, yawning wider and wider until its lips ultimately folded back and it swallowed itself. I looked down— beneath my feet the chaos continued. Geometric shapes rolled and tumbled, changing into different forms or merging into one another; colors pulsed; the air carried the scents of honey, turpentine, roses . . . it was like a 3-D collaboration between Salvador Dalí, Picasso and Jackson Pollock. With a liberal dose of Heironymus Bosch and the really cool old Warner Bros. cartoons thrown in for good measure.

So much for pleading insanity, I realized. I truly wasn't lying on a gurney watching a mind movie while waiting for some doctor to put a padded stick in my mouth and pump enough volts through my skull to revive the Frankenstein monster. Nope. This was *real*. It had to be. No one, sane or insane, could imagine all this.

It wasn't just my eyes that were overwhelmed. There was a continuous cacophony going on—things creaking, bells tolling, chasms yawning, pits slurping. . . . I stopped trying to identify all the sounds, just as I gave up trying to see everything going on. I'd need eyes not just in the back of my head but on top of it and in the soles of my shoes as well.

And the smells! I was staggered by a searingly intense whiff of peppermint, followed by the smell of hot copper. Most of them I couldn't identify. A hefty portion of the sights, sounds and smells were synesthetic—I could hear colors, could see tastes. Old Mr. Telfilm down the street claimed to be synesthetic, and was constantly telling anyone who would listen about how sharp the sky smelled or how the taste of pasta was turquoise and sounded C flat. Now, finally, I knew what he meant.

I realized that Jay had hold of my arm with his good one and was shaking it. "Joey! Listen up—we've got to get moving. You don't have protective gear—you won't last long in the In-Between without it."

"The what?" I reluctantly turned my attention away from what looked like really neat graphic imagery—huge towers forming and rising, only to melt into quicksilver lakes and start over. Jay grabbed me and fastened his metal gaze on mine. "We've got to go! I can't get us back to InterWorld Prime with my arm messed up this way. The pain is too distracting, and any drugs I take will make it too hard for me to concentrate. You'll have to find the way through."

I looked at him in utter astonishment. About fifty feet away a trapezoid chased and cornered a smaller rhomboid, then "ate" it by leisurely flowing around and over it. Directly above me an ordinary casement window suddenly appeared out of nowhere. Its curtains peeled back and the window slid up, revealing a howling blackness beyond it from which issued piteous screams, groans and cries. It was either an open window on Hell, I decided, or a look inside my own mind at this point.

I didn't know which was worse.

"How can I find the way through this—this—what did you call it?"

"The In-Between," Jay said, his voice muffled through the metal mask. He was holding his injured arm with his other one now. The wound wasn't bleeding much, but it definitely looked like it needed more than a few Band-Aids. "It's the interstitial folds between the various planes of reality. Call it 'hyperspace' or a 'wormhole,' if you want. Or it's the dark spaces between the convolutions in your brain or the place where the magician keeps the rabbit before he pulls it out of his hat. Okay? It really doesn't matter what you call it—what matters is getting through it and back to InterWorld Prime. *That's* what you've got to do, Joey."

"You've really got the wrong guy," I tried to tell him. "I couldn't find the back of my hand if you wrote directions on my palm."

"Because your talent doesn't lie in navigating the planes—it lies in navigating *between* them. And that's where we are now. Pay attention," he continued, overriding me when I tried to interrupt. "The In-Between is a dangerous place. There are—creatures—that live here, or partly here. We call 'em 'mudluffs.' That's an acronym, MDLF, standing for multidimensional life-form. Which is kind of a pointless label, I know—we're all multidimensional life-forms, right? Except that you and I can only move freely in three dimensions and linearly in a fourth, whereas they have complete freedom in who knows how many. Including, in many cases, the fourth."

Now, most of what he was saying was going so far over my head that I feared for local air traffic. But I'd seen *Twilight Zone* reruns, and I knew what the fourth dimension was. "You mean they can travel in time?"

"We think some can. It's hard to tell, because there's a certain temporal flexibility between the planes that can affect all of us. You learn to compensate for it when you Walk—otherwise you can spend a month on one world and find that only a couple of days have gone by in another one. It gets real confusing real fast, so we try to take advantage of it only when absolutely necessary.

"But that's not important now. My point was the mudluffs—stay away from them. They aren't intelligent, but they can be dangerous. Usually they stay in the In-Between, but some of 'em know how to squeeze out, like polydimensional toothpaste, into the various worlds."

I was feeling pretty overwhelmed by all this, and starting to wonder how much of what Jay was telling me was real and how much was just him yanking my chain. "Right. Next you'll be telling me they're the ones responsible for all the legends of fairies, goblins, like that," I said. I expected Jay to laugh, but he shook his head.

"No, those are usually HEX scouts. Binary scouts tend to be seen as 'gray men' and all that other Roswell crap. But I think some of the tales of demons probably began with mud-luffs. But you'll get all that in your basic Altiverse studies. All that matters now is making sure we don't run into any of 'em, and getting out of the way if you do." He grabbed me, turned me and gave me a push. "What're you waiting for? Shock's pretty much worn off for me, and this hexburn is starting to *hurt*. I want a hot bath and a bloodstream full of painkillers. So pick 'em up and put 'em down, Walker! You know the way! Hit it!"

I started to tell him again that he had the wrong guy—but then I stopped. I looked ahead of us, into that crazy swirling Mandelbrot brew called the In-Between, and somehow I realized he was right.

I *did* know the way.

I don't know how I knew—I don't even know how I knew that I knew. But the route was there, clear and shining in my head. It wasn't self-deception this time either. This was the real thing.

Simultaneously with that realization, I knew something else—that Jay was right about the mudluffs. There were critters out there that would make two bites each of us and use our leg bones for toothpicks. I didn't want to run into any of them, and the longer we stayed in the In-Between, the greater the risk of doing that became. They could track us down with senses we don't even have names for.

I started moving, and Jay followed. He hopped onto my purple pathway and we stuck to it for a while, ducking under writhing Möbius strips and pulsating Klein bottles. Gravity—or whatever the force that kept us on the path was—seemed to be off and on. When I realized that the time had come to leave the purple ramp, the only way to do so was to jump off. That took some guts, if I do say so—it looked like I was jumping into an abyss that made the dive off the ship seem puny by comparison. But the way was shining bright and clear in my head, so I held my breath and stepped off.

My stomach tried to claw its way up my throat and escape, the entire In-Between rotated ninety degrees in several directions at once—and then "down" wasn't down anymore. I floated among the lazily drifting geometric forms, past what looked like a partly open wardrobe that gave a glimpse of an inner door leading to a wondrous, sun-warmed land, and continued following the map in my head toward what looked like a vortex of some sort.

Jay was right behind me. This wasn't a true weightless state, evidently—big surprise, considering our surroundings—because I had read somewhere that trying to swim in zero g got you nowhere fast; all the movements just canceled out. You needed to pull yourself along with hand- and footholds, or—better yet—have some kind of propulsion.

We had neither, and yet we sailed along just fine, seemingly propelled by nothing more than innate righteousness. But I started to get nervous when I realized that our route lay into that lazily swirling whirlpool or maelstrom or tornado or whatever it was called—you run out of words pretty quickly in the In-Between.

Jay was right behind me, and when I stopped—it required nothing more than mentally putting on the brakes—he collided gently with me from behind. "What's wrong, Joey?"

"That's what's wrong." I pointed at the rotating funnel, realizing as I did so that I hadn't the faintest idea what it was made of. Not surprising; I didn't know what nine tenths of the stuff in the In-Between was made of. Dark matter, possibly—that would explain a lot. Wouldn't it?

But I didn't care if it was made out of tapioca pudding. I had no desire to dive headlong into that funnel. There had to be easier ways to get to Oz.

Jay looked "down" into the funnel. It seemed to stretch out forever inside, and the swirling convolutions flickered occasionally with what might be lightning. "Is it the way out?"

"I—yeah. It is." There was no sense trying to hedge. It might as well have had a big, bright neon sign blinking EXIT.

Jay said, in that voice that was still so maddeningly familiar, "Some things are the same no matter which world you're in, kid. One of 'em is this: The quickest way out of something is usually straight through it." And with that he floated past me and dived into the vortex.

He either fell or was sucked in; either way it was fast. His body seemed to diminish in size much faster than it should—there was a weird forced perspective aspect to it that I didn't like at all. What if it were some kind of singularity? All that might be left of Jay—and me, if I followed him—would be a line of subatomic particles stretched out like an infinitely long string of beads.

But it seemed my only other choice was to stay here in wackyland, and that didn't seem like a real viable alternative. Jay had saved my life—I had to at least try to return the favor.

I took a deep gulp of whatever passed for air in the In-Between and dove in.

CHAPTER SEVEN

I fell out of a shimmering patch of sky about six feet above the ground. Jay had had the good sense to roll out of the way when he landed, so I hit the dirt hard enough to knock the wind out of me.

Jay hauled me over onto my back, made sure that my windpipe wasn't obstructed, then sat cross-legged beside me and waited. After a couple of minutes my lungs remembered their job and got back to it, albeit grumpily.

Jay waited until I was breathing normally again, then handed me a small flask. I don't know where he kept it—that formfitting mirror suit he wore looked like it didn't leave room for a book of matches. I looked at the flask rather uncertainly, then handed it back. "Thanks, but I don't drink."

He didn't accept the flask. "Now might be a good time to start. There's a lot you need to know, and some of it won't be easy to hear." When I still didn't take it, he said, "I mean it, Joey. You haven't had time for shock to set in yet; but it's coming like a freight train, and you're tied to the tracks." An idea seemed to occur to him then; he leaned forward and stared at me from behind that blank silver oval of a mask. "Wait a minute—you think there's *alcohol* in this?" When I nodded, he burst out laughing.

"By the Arc, that's funny. Joey, trust me—this stuff is to alcohol what penicillin is to snake oil. Why in the name of all that's sane would we drink a teratogenic poison when there are so many other ways to construct ethyl molecules that don't have devastating side effects?" He opened the flask, saluted me with it and took a swig. What fascinated me was that he didn't take off that featureless mask—the golden liquid flowed *through* it. It seemed to swirl around just beneath a transparent membrane on the lower half—the gold drink mixing with the silver whatever in Rorschach patterns—and then faded away. Then he handed me the flask once more and this time I took a drink.

When I retire, don't bother giving me a pension—just let me have a little tavern on a world somewhere in the middle span of the Arc and give me license to sell this stuff. It eased down my throat and cuddled up in my stomach as gently as if it had lived there all its life, and from there a sensation of relaxation, strength and confidence radiated outward that made every part of me, up to and including finger- and toenails, feel like the last son of Krypton. I wanted to leap a tall building in a single bound, juggle Volkswagens and come up with a unified field theory—and then move on to something challenging. What I did was hand the flask back to Jay. "Wow."

"Goes down smooth," Jay agreed. "There's a world out near the inner edge of the HEX Hegemony, and on that world is a lake, and in that lake is an island, and on that island is a tree. Once every seven years that tree fruits, and it's considered one of InterWorld's most honored jobs for a team to be picked to Walk there and come back with baskets full of them apples. They're the secret ingredient of this little pick-me-up." He stood up. "Be right back. Gotta see a man about a horse." He moved off about a hundred feet or so and stood with his back to me.

I wondered why he hadn't gone behind a rock—then, as I looked around for the first time since I fell out of the In-Between, I realized there was no rock big enough. We were in the middle of a dusty plain that stretched to the horizon in every direction. A ring of distant mountains surrounded the plain, turning it into the punch bowl of the gods. I wondered how hot it got here, and glanced up at the sky, looking for the sun.

There was no sun.

There was no sky, really. Instead, colors swirled and flowed like oil on water, a psychedelic light show stretching from horizon to horizon. There was no single source of light, but everything was nonetheless lit by some subtle, unlocatable radiance.

I glanced over at where Jay stood. Now he seemed to be

talking to something he held in one hand. A recorder, most likely. Faint snatches of words came to me every now and then, but none of them were understandable. I felt vaguely uneasy—was he recording what I'd done as evidence for some kind of kangaroo court? Was he really my friend? Sure, he'd saved my life, but was it just so his side could have me rather than Lady Indigo's? I seemed to be a pretty valuable property—though for the life of me I couldn't figure out why. All through school I'd been the last one picked for teams; even bullies like Ted Russell picked on me only as a last resort, after they'd beaten up everyone else.

I shrugged away the momentary paranoia. I trusted Jay. I wasn't really sure why. There was just something about him.

After a few more minutes he came back. "Okay, pull up a rock, 'cause this'll take a while," he said, following his own advice. "Let's start big and work our way down."

"Why not start at the beginning?" I suggested.

"Two reasons. Imprimus: There is no real beginning to this little tale and probably no end either. Secondus: It's my story and I'll start wherever I darn well please."

There didn't seem to be much argument I could offer against that, so I leaned back against a rocky outcropping and waited. "Couldn't you take that mask off?"

"No. Not yet. Okay, the whole picture is what we call the Altiverse. Not to be confused with the Multiverse, which means the entire infinity of parallel universes and all the worlds therein. The Altiverse is that slice of the Multiverse that contains all the myriad Earths. And there are a *lot* of 'em." He paused, and I got the feeling he was frowning at me. "You understand quantum differentiation? Heisenberg's uncertainty principle? Multiple world lines?"

"Uh . . ." We'd touched on some of it in Mr. Lerner's science class, and I remembered reading an article on the *Discover* website. Plus I'd seen that episode of classic *Trek* where Spock had a beard and the *Enterprise* was full of space pirates. But all that put together made me about as much of an expert as the family cat.

I said as much; Jay waved it off. "Doesn't matter. You'll pick up what you need to know—cultural osmosis. The thing to remember is that certain decisions—important ones, those that can create major ripples in the time stream—can cause alternate worlds to splinter off into divergent space-time continua. Remember this, or you'll wind up paralyzed every time you have to make a choice: The Altiverse is *not* going to create a brave new world based on your decision to wear green socks today instead of red ones. Or if it does, that world will only last a few femtoseconds before being recycled into the reality it split off from. But if your president is trying to decide whether or not to carpet bomb some Middle East saber rattler, he gets it both ways—because two worlds are created where before there was one.

Of course, the In-Between keeps them apart, so he'll never know."

"Wait a minute—it sounds like you're trying to say that the creation of new alternate worlds is a *conscious* decision."

"I'm not *trying* to say it—I just said it. Or weren't you paying attention?"

"But *whose* consciousness? God's?"

Jay shrugged, and the molten colors of the sky swam and ran on his gleaming shoulders. "It's physics, not theology. Call it what you want—God, Buddha, the Flying Spaghetti Monster, Prime Mover Unmoved. The totality of everything. I don't care. Consciousness is a factor in *every* aspect of the Multiverse. Quantum math needs a viewpoint, or it doesn't work. Just try to remember not to confuse consciousness with ego. Two completely different things—and of the two, ego's the disposable one."

I wanted to ask him more questions about that, but he was already moving on. "Think of that slice of the Multiverse as an arc—with several extra dimensions, of course." He made gestures that looked like he was strangling a snake. "At each extreme of the arc are the homeworlds of two hegemonies— empires that each control a small percentage of the individual Earths in the arc. One of them we call the Binary. They use advanced technology—by 'advanced' I mean compared to what most of the other Earths have come up with—to radiate out along the arc, conquering as they go. You nearly met up with a couple of representatives back on that Earth you'd Walked to—the 'opposition is nonproductive' boys on those flying disks. They love saying things like that. The other empire calls itself HEX. Their artillery relies on magic—spells, talismans, sacrifices—"

"Whoa." I held up two flat palms in a T shape—the time-out gesture. "Hold up, hold up. *Magic*? You mean like 'abra-cadabra'? 'hocus-pocus'?"

Jay's body language indicated annoyance, but his tone was patient. "Well, I've never actually heard one of them *say* 'hocus-pocus,' but, yeah, that's the general idea."

I felt like my brain was leaking out of my ears. "But that's not—"

"Possible? You sure looked like a believer to me when I pulled you off the *Lacrimae Mundi*."

I opened my mouth, then decided to shut it again when nothing came out. Jay leaned back with an attitude of relief. "Good. For a moment I thought you were going rational on me. Always remember: In an infinity of worlds, anything is not only possible, it's *mandatory*.

"To continue: The Binary and HEX are locked in strug-gle, both overt and covert, for the ultimate control of the Altiverse. They've been going at it for centuries, making real slow headway because of the sheer magnitude of the task. I think the last census we intercepted indicated somewhere in the neighborhood of several million billion trillions of

Earths—with more of 'em popping out of the vacuum faster than bubbles in champagne.

"There's a Council of Thirteen that rules HEX, and the Binary is run by an artificial intelligence that calls itself 01101. Each of them wants only one thing—to run the whole shebang. What they refuse to accept is that the Altiverse functions best when the forces of magic and science are in balance. And that's where InterWorld comes in."

"You mentioned it—or them—before."

"Right. That's who I work for—that's where you're leading us."

He stopped for a breath. I had more questions than there were Earths, but before I could ask them and before he could resume speaking, we heard something roar.

It was a distant sound, unlike anything I'd ever heard before—but it was definitely the sound of a hunting beast, and probably one big enough to look at both Jay and me as blue plate specials. Jay hopped to his feet. "Come on." Even with the mask on he looked nervous. "This world is still on the cusp of the In-Between, and that's way too close for me."

We started walking at a brisk pace across the baked and cracked valley floor. What baked it? I wondered. The temperature was comfortable, even a little bracing—I estimated in the mid-sixties or thereabouts. I glanced up at that crawling sky, and it didn't look fascinating anymore. It looked like those colors could come pouring down on us at any moment, like boiling lead cascading from battlements. I shuddered and walked a little faster.

One good thing about where we were—nothing could sneak up on us. But I still didn't like it. We were as exposed as a couple of field mice in a hockey rink. We walked and walked, and those mountains didn't look any closer.

Then I noticed a flicker of color out of the corner of my eye.

I looked over to one side and saw something that brought me to a stop. At first glance it looked like a huge soap bubble—I mean big, the size of a basketball—drifting out of a large ground fissure. But it only drifted so high, and then it stopped and bobbled around like a balloon trying to escape its tether.

"What's that?" I asked.

Jay turned his silver-coated head toward the bubble. I was standing far enough away that I could see my whole body reflected along the curve of his cheek and jawline. "Beats me. Never saw anything like it. Got to be a mudluff of some kind, though—which means we assume it's dangerous and walk away." He started to walk again, and, after a last glance at the bubble—*It almost looks alive*, I thought—I turned to follow Jay.

There was a rattling noise somewhere in the distance. It made me think of rattlesnakes or of someone dragging a huge length of chain over rocks.

I turned around and looked, because that was where the sound had come from. I didn't see anything that looked capable of making that kind of racket. What I did see was the little bubble straining frantically this way and that, as if trying to escape something. Its spherical surface pulsed rapidly with variegated colors—mostly dark reds and oranges shading to purple.

It was scared. I'm not sure how I knew, but it was real clear to me that the little thing was in some kind of distress.

I turned and headed over toward the crevasse.

Behind me I heard Jay shout, *"Joey! No! Come back!"*

"I think it's in trouble!" I called back. "It's not dangerous." And I kept going.

I came to a stop near the crevasse, which was closer and bigger than I'd thought it would be. The bubble creature, I could now see, was somehow tethered to the rocks at the edge of the chasm by a thin line of protoplasm or ectoplasm or something.

"Joey! That thing's an In-Betweener! A mudluff! Get back here right now!"

I pretended I couldn't hear him.

The strand was clear and thin, like a line of saliva. It didn't look like it would take much more than a mean look to sever it and free the little bubble creature.

"It's been tied up!" I called to Joey. "I think I can free it."

He was coming toward me. If I was going to do this, I was

going to have to do it fast. I reached out and tugged on the line. It was stronger than it looked.

"Hey," I called to Jay. "Have you got a knife? I bet we could cut this." He didn't reply. Even through the silver suit I could tell he was mad.

The little bubble creature above us seemed agitated. I let go of the line. It was slightly sticky. I found myself thinking of a spider's web.

"I know he's harmless," I told Jay. "Look at him."

Jay sighed. He was maybe five, six feet away from me. "You may be right," he said. "But there's something about this whole thing that seems wrong. How do you think the little guy got stuck there? And why?"

The strand of web began to vibrate. Then there was a roar so loud that it nearly shattered my eardrums, and I realized that I'd summoned something by pulling on the strand of web. I thought I'd been trying to free the little mudluff, but I'd actually been banging a dinner gong.

A monster reared up out of the abyss.

"Monster" is an overused word, I know, but nothing else applies here. It had a head that looked a bit like a shark's and a bit like a tyrannosaur's, mounted on a centipede-like body as thick as a delivery van. I don't know how long it was, but it was long enough to rise out of what looked like a bottomless chasm; and as each segment came sliding up the rock, it rattled and echoed through the gorge like a huge length of chain. In a lot less time than it takes to tell this, it had risen to a good thirty feet above the edge. It stared down at me with enormous compound eyes, each as big as my hand.

Then it struck.

Its head was the size of my dad's cab; and its mouth gaped open, revealing jaws lined with multiple rows of teeth, each as long as a steak knife. For all its size it dropped toward me like an express elevator. I was just about to become an hors d'oeuvre when I felt someone smash into me from behind, hurling me forward to sprawl on the edge.

I twisted onto my back and stared—stared at Jay standing in the spot where I had stood just an instant before. Then the huge gaping maw of the beast enveloped him, started to close—

And then that little soap bubble came shooting in from over my shoulder. I realized I must've broken the strand that had anchored it when I fell. It hit the monster's muzzle, splattering over it like translucent goop.

The monster reared back with a roar of rage, dropping Jay's body. Its mouth was still open—those deadly jaws hadn't had time to close fully on him, and now it had to keep its jaws open to breathe, because the mudluff had covered its nose with the clinging translucent substance of his body. The monster thrashed about, roaring in frustration as it tried to shake the amoebalike mudluff loose. It succeeded in flinging blobs of the thing's substance, tethered by elastic tendrils, a few feet away, only to have them snap back and replaster themselves around its nose. Hard as it was to believe, that blob of transparent Silly Putty was actually keeping the Midgard serpent from chowing down on Jay and me!

The monster dropped back below ground level and, from the sounds and the way the ground shook repeatedly, was trying to scrape the In-Betweener off by battering its scaly snout against the rocks. I didn't wait to find out which one would win. Instead I ran over to Jay, grabbed his arms and dragged him, stumbling and leaning on me, away from the action. I figured that overgrown soap bubble wasn't going to last long.

I stopped a good five hundred yards away. Jay sat down hard on the sand. The roars and tremors from the now-unseen monster continued. I could see clouds of dust and occasional rock fragments being hurled into view. It would have been funny except for one other thing I now noticed: a trail of blood, thick as paint and wide as my hand, stretching unbroken from the edge of the chasm back to Jay's body.

I gasped and knelt quickly beside him. The silver suit had been pierced through on either side of his body—two brutal punctures on his left side, three on his right, just above his hips. The monster's teeth had each left holes over an inch in diameter, and Jay's blood was pumping from them. There was no way to stop it, and I don't know if it would have done any good anyway—he'd already lost so much blood.

Weakly he held up a hand, which I grasped.

"I'll get you back to InterWorld," I said, not knowing what else to do or say. "We'll go through the In-Between— it won't take long—I—I'm so sorry—"

"Save it," Jay whispered. "It . . . won't work. I'm bleeding . . . like three . . . stuck pigs. And I think the thing is venomous. You wouldn't believe . . . how much it hurts. . . ." His voice was muffled and dull.

"What can I do?" I asked helplessly.

"Put my hand on . . . the sand," he said. "Got to show you . . . how to go . . . the final distance. . . ."

I put his hand down on the ground. He drew something in spastic, jerking movements in the sand.

Then he stopped and seemed to be resting. I felt utterly useless.

"Jay?" I said. "You'll be fine. Really, you will." I wasn't lying. I was saying it, hoping that by saying it I was somehow going to make it so.

He surprised me by shoving himself up to rest on one elbow—his other hand grabbed my shirtfront and dragged me with surprising strength down until my face was only an inch away from his mask. Once again I looked into the wavering reflection of my own features, grotesquely mirrored in the suit's surface.

"Tell . . . the Old Man . . . sorry . . . made him . . . short one operative. Tell him . . . my replacement . . . gets my highest . . . recommendation."

"I'll tell him, whoever he is," I promised. "But will you do me one favor in return?" He feebly cocked his head at a questioning angle.

"Take off your mask," I said. "Let me see who you are."

He hesitated, then he raised one hand to his face, prodded the suit material just under the chin with a finger. The material covering his head changed from reflective silver to a dull gunmetal gray and sort of shrank back into a ring around his neck.

I stared. It hadn't made any difference. The mask was still in place. At least, that was my initial thought, brought on by the shock of seeing Jay's face.

It was my own face, of course. But not exactly. Jay looked to be at least five years older than me. There was a splotch of scar tissue across his right cheek, and the lower part of his ear was knuckled with keloid growth as well. But there weren't nearly enough scars to hide who he was.

He was me. That was why that voice had been so familiar. It was my voice. Or rather, it was what my voice might sound like in five years.

I wondered why I had not known all along, and I realized that, on some level, I had. Of course he was me. Cooler and braver and wiser than me. And he'd given his life to save me.

He looked at me with eyes dulling. "Get . . . moving . . ."

His whisper was barely audible. "Can't lose . . . a single operative now . . . too dangerous. Tell him . . . FrostNight . . . comes. . . ."

"I will, I promise," I said. But his eyes had closed. He was unconscious.

It didn't matter. A promise was binding, whether Jay heard me make it or not. *I* had heard me make it, and I didn't want to live the rest of my life trying to justify to myself why I hadn't done the right thing.

I lowered his body and rocked back on my heels, feeling a sudden lump in my throat. I'm not sure how long I stood there, just breathing.

Then I looked down at the figures he had drawn in the sand.

It had to be important. But when I looked closely at the characters, they made no sense. It seemed to be some kind of mathematical equation:

$$\{IW\}:=\Omega/\infty$$

I didn't understand what it meant, but the symbols seemed to take root in my brain, glowing in my mind's eye.

It was quiet in that rocky place. I could hear Jay's gasping breaths and the hiss of the windblown sand and nothing else. I didn't know how long it had been that way, but I knew that unequal battle between the dinomonster and the little mudluff could have ended only one way. I felt sorry for the little soap bubble thing: first bait in a trap, then killed trying to save Jay and me from a monster.

I stood, turned and looked back. There was no sign of either critter. I took a few cautious steps forward, trying to get a better view.

Nothing but settling dust . . .

Jay's skin was changing color, taking on a bluish tint. There must have been venom on that creature's teeth, like he'd said. And if I'd listened to him, and not been stupid, he would never have put himself into the jaws of death, trying to get me out of them. I'd rushed in where angels probably really did fear to tread—and Jay was dying because of that. Because of me. It was my fault. There was no one else to blame.

I looked up at the sky, and I made another promise, to anything that was out there, anyone who was listening, that if Jay lived, if he pulled through this, if I got him medical attention and he was fine, then I'd be the best, hardest-working, nicest, coolest person anyone could ever be. I'd be St. Francis of Assisi and Gautama Buddha and everyone else like that.

But his eyes were closed, and he was not breathing, or moving, now, and it didn't matter what I promised or how good I was going to be in the future or anything.

Nothing mattered.

He was dead.

CHAPTER EIGHT

I couldn't leave him there.

You're going to laugh at me, but I couldn't. It might have been the sensible thing to do—maybe if I could have dug a grave or something, I would have felt okay about leaving Jay in the desert at the borders of the edge of the In-Between. But the ground was baked, hard red mud with a thin layer of sand over it.

So I tried to pull him. He didn't budge. I knew that he outweighed me, but even so, I'd helped him drag himself away from the chasm's edge not ten minutes ago—and probably used up every ounce of adrenaline in my system doing it, I now realized. Now that the danger was over, I had about as much chance of moving him as I had of raising the *Titanic* with my teeth.

I wondered if it was the metal suit that weighed him down so. I examined it, looking for a catch or a zipper or something.

Nothing.

There was a hushing noise beside me and I turned. It was the little In-Betweener. The mudluff creature was hovering in the air beside me, floating in space like an amoeba the size of a cat, glittering with all the colors of a rainbow.

"Hey," I said. "Well, at least you're okay. But Jay's dead. Maybe I ought to have left you there with that tyrannosaurus thing after all."

The soap bubble color changed to a rather miserable shade of purple.

"I didn't mean it," I said. "But he was . . . my friend. He was *me*, kind of. And now he's dead, and I can't even get him back to his home. He's too heavy."

The purple color warmed up until the thing glowed a gentle shade of gold. It extended something that wasn't quite a limb and wasn't really a tentacle—a pseudopod, I suppose, if that means what I think it does—and it touched the metal suit just above the heart.

"Yes," I said. "He's dead."

It pulsed gold—a sort of frustrated gold—and tapped exactly the same place on the suit.

"You want me to touch it there?"

It changed color once more, to a serene blue, a *pleased* sort of blue. I put my finger where the pseudopod had been, and the suit opened to me like a flower to the sun. Jay had been wearing gray boxer shorts and a green T-shirt underneath it. His body seemed so pale. I dragged the suit out from underneath him.

It weighed a ton. Well, maybe a hundred pounds. The

amoeba was still hanging around, as if it were trying to tell me something. It extended a scarlet-tipped pseudopod toward the silver mass of the suit, which lay crumpled on the red earth. Then it pointed at me, and twinkling silver veins appeared across its balloon body.

"What?" I asked, frustrated. "I wish you could talk."

It pointed at the silver suit, now faded to a dull, battleship gray, and then back at me once more.

"You think I should put it on?"

It glowed blue, the same shade of blue it had gone before. *Yes. I should put it on.* "I've heard of speaking in tongues," I said. "I've never heard of speaking in colors."

Then I picked up the suit—now something like a starfish-shaped overcoat—and draped it over me. It hung there heavily and made my back hurt. It felt like a lead-lined blanket. It was cold and dead. There was no way I could walk more than a dozen steps in any direction wearing this.

"Now what?" I asked the amoeba. It turned a puzzled shade of green, and yellows and crimsons chased across its surface in rapid succession. Then it pointed, hesitantly, to a spot on the middle of the suit, over my chest. I touched it.

Nothing happened.

I touched it again. I banged it. I rubbed it. I squeezed it between finger and thumb as tightly as I could—and suddenly the lead blanket that was covering me came to life. It flowed and oozed and ran over my body, covering me from legs to head. My vision went dark when it flowed across my face. I felt a moment of pure, suffocating panic—and then I could see once more, better than before, and breathe as well.

Looking down at my body, I could see the silver covering, but I could also see *inside* it. It was a little like the heads-up displays fighter pilots use in their cockpits. I could see the golden bottle and what looked like a gun of sorts and several objects I didn't recognize. They seemed to be in pockets of some kind. And I could see my own body.

I was warm now, except my left shoulder, where the suit had been damaged by Lady Indigo's spell, and the places where it had been punctured.

Seen through the mirror mask, the amoeba thing looked even stranger. It was like looking at something huge through binoculars held the wrong way. It was only the size of a cat— I knew that. But somehow I could not shake the idea that it was truly the size of a skyscraper, only it was ten miles away. Does that make any sense?

"Do you have a name?" I asked it.

It glowed a hundred colors. I took that as a yes. Trouble is, I don't speak colors. "I'm going to call you Hue," I told him. "It's a joke. Not a funny one, the other kind." It glowed gold, which I took as it not minding.

I bent down, picked Jay up and put him over my shoulders. I could still feel the bulk of him, but it felt like the suit was taking most of the weight. It felt like he weighed about thirty pounds.

And then I thought:

$$\{IW\}:=\Omega/\infty$$

—and I made for the base, carrying Jay's body over my shoulders like a Sioux hunter carrying a deer back to camp.

Hue bobbed along in the air beside me for a little way, until I came to a path that I could feel would lead me into the Earth with the InterWorld base in it.

I wish I could explain it better than that. I could feel it there, in the same way you can feel with your tongue a place in your tooth where a filling has fallen out. I could *feel* it.

It was time to Walk. And I did.

The last thing I saw of that place was Hue, bobbing maybe a bit sadly in the air behind me. And then the scene was replaced by . . .

Nothing . . .

A riverbank . . .

A glimpse of a city . . .

A thousand eyes, each closing and opening independently, each looking for me . . .

A grassy plain and, in the distance, purplish mountains.

And suddenly I was there, wherever "there" was. I knew it. I could feel it in my head.

$$\{IW\}:=\Omega/\infty$$

wasn't going to take me any farther.

But there wasn't anything around. I was in the middle of

a deserted pampas, all on my own. I put Jay's body down on the grassy ground. I figured that either the people from Jay's base—from InterWorld, whatever that was—would come and find me or they wouldn't, and suddenly and honestly I didn't care one way or the other.

I put my finger to the soft place under my chin and felt the suit retract from my face, leaving it naked to the warm air. And then, all alone, a million million miles from everywhere, I started to cry—for Jay, and for my parents, and for Jenny and the squid, and for Rowena and Ted Russell and Mr. Dimas and all of us.

But mostly I cried for me.

I cried and sobbed until there wasn't anything left inside me to cry with, and then I sat there, with the tears drying on my face, feeling empty and wrung out until the sun went down, and a city in a glass dome came over the pampas, levitating silently about six feet above the ground. It stopped fifty feet away from Jay and me, and a party of people who looked kind of like me came over and picked us up and took us away.

PART II

PART II

CHAPTER NINE

I was holding onto the side of the cliff face for dear life. I was wearing a one-piece gray coverall and a pair of climbing boots. There was a rope clipped to the belt around my waist, attached to the climber maybe twenty feet above me. She disliked me cordially. Which complicated matters somewhat, seeing that a hundred feet above her was freedom and warmth and solid food and a way back to base.

The way I felt, a hundred feet might as well have been a hundred miles. I was hungry and cold and my fingers hurt, and so did my toes. Not to mention everything in between.

I had a neural-net band around my head, coded to stop me Walking out of this if an opportunity presented. Which I might have done. Believe me, it was tempting, especially when the sleet started: a wet, freezing rain with snow mixed in, which soaked me to the skin and then froze me. Perfect. I started shivering so hard I could barely hold on.

There was a cough just behind me. I turned, very carefully.

It was Jai. He was one of the ones who looked a lot like me, except his skin was walnut brown. He wore a one-piece white robe and was sitting cross-legged. Actually he was floating cross-legged, about a hundred and fifty feet above the ground.

"I came to inquire how you were faring," he told me in his gentle accent. "This rain makes the climb quite problematic. Should you desire to terminate the ascent at this juncture, it would not be perceived as something lacking in you."

My teeth were rattling like dice in a cup; I could barely hear him. "What?"

"Do you want to stop now?"

Like I said, it was tempting. But I had more than enough problems without being labeled a coward as well. "I'll keep going," I told him, "if it kills me."

"That," he said disapprovingly, "is *not* an option." Jai was something of a jerk, but at least he acknowledged that I existed. He floated slowly upward to the camp at the top of the hill.

I started climbing again. I reached a deep crack in the rock, which I chimneyed up, removing most of the skin from my arms and back in the process. After what seemed only a small eternity I reached a ledge about thirty feet above the place I had been, and I saw the girl I was climbing with. She was huddled on one side of the shelf, out of the direct reach of the sleet. She couldn't have been comfortable, though, a fact which I tried not to take too much pleasure in. She barely spared me a glance when I got there. She was staring out into the sky.

"Got any plans for reaching the top?" I asked her, eyeing the rock face above us warily.

"The list of people I don't talk to is pretty short," she told me. "Actually, you're about it." She went back to looking at the featureless storm.

Well, okay . . . I thumbed open the thermopack hanging from my belt and poured out a cupful of steaming hot reconstituted buffalo soup. I didn't offer her any; first, because she had her own packs hanging from her own belt, just like mine, and second, because to hell with her.

I sipped the soup slowly, so as not to burn my mouth— that stuff got hot *fast*—and looked at Jo, particularly at the two things that made her so different from me.

"Stop staring."

"I'm sorry," I said. "It's just, where I come from, nobody has wings."

She looked at me as if I were something she'd just found on the sole of her shoe. Jo's from one of the magic worlds. The wings—huge, white, feathered wings, like angels have in paintings—don't keep her aloft when she flies, although she can use them to glide and to steer herself. What keeps her up when she flies, the Old Man once said, is the conviction that she *can* fly. That and the fact that on her world there truly is magic in the air. I'd often wanted to ask her if her people descended from winged apes, like Jakon's folk

95

came from a wolfish sort of world, or if, long ago in her world, some sorcerer grafted swan wings onto the back of a baby and they just took it from there. But, since she viewed me with about the same degree of affection she might an Ebola virus, it wasn't likely I'd ever find out.

I'd been at the camp ten days, and it already seemed like a lifetime. And not a happy lifetime. Rather, it was one of those lifetimes that convinces you you must have been Genghis Khan in a previous incarnation, and you were still paying off the karmic debt.

Ten days before being on the cliff in the rain, I'd woken up on some kind of canvas camp bed in a white room that smelled like disinfectant with the sound of band music in the background. It was a mournful sort of music, stirring yet sad.

It was a funeral march.

The music stopped. I got out of the bed and walked, a little unsteadily, over to the window and looked out.

There were about five hundred people standing on a large parade ground. Very different people. They were standing in lines, arrayed around a box. On the box was a body covered with a black flag.

I knew who the body belonged to.

And I knew whose life he had died saving.

Up on a dais was a man who looked kind of like I might, if I lived to middle age. He was just finishing saying good things about Jay, I knew, although I could barely hear his words.

And then the people started to shout. They shouted in five hundred different voices, a wordless shout that was a wail of loss but also a cheer of victory. It was shouted and screamed and wailed and torn from five hundred throats.

And the box with the coffin in it flickered and shimmered and shifted. And then it flared and was completely gone.

The band started to play again, the mournful march, but this time it was more upbeat. *Life goes on* was what it said.

I went back and sat on the canvas bed. I was in some kind of hospital. That was obvious. And I was in the bubble-dome base. And I had seen Jay's funeral.

There was a knock on the door.

"Come in," I said.

It was the older man, the one who'd given the speech. "Hello, Joey," he said. His uniform was crisp and clean. "Welcome to Base Town." One of his eyes was brown, just like mine. The other was artificial: it was like a cluster of colored LEDs where his eye ought to be.

"You're me, too," I said.

He inclined his head. It might have been a nod of agreement. "Joe Harker. Around here they call me the Old Man, mostly behind my back. I run this place."

"I'm sorry about Jay," I said. "I brought back his body."

"That was well done," he said. "And you brought back his

encounter suit, which was even more important. We only have a dozen of them. They don't make them anymore. The world that manufactured them is . . . gone now." He paused.

I figured I had to say something, so I said, "Gone? A whole world?"

"Worlds are cheap, Joey. It sounds horrible to say, but most horrible things have a measure of truth in them. The Binary and HEX consider worlds very cheap indeed, and life cheaper still. . . . But let's get back to you. You did well, bringing back the body. It gave us something to say goodbye to. And the suit contained his last messages." He paused again. "Do you remember when we brought you in? You seemed more or less delirious. You kept calling for me."

"I did?"

"You did. You told us that you'd got Jay killed, saving you. All about the MDLF and the tyrannosaur snake. That you were stupid and got him into trouble."

I looked down. "Yeah."

He flipped open a notebook, checked it. "'Jay said to say sorry to the Old Man, to tell him he was sorry he had made him short one operative. He said his replacement gets his highest recommendation.'"

"Did I tell you that?"

"Yes." He looked back at his notebook. Then he said in a puzzled tone, "What's FrostNight?"

"FrostNight? I don't know. It was something that Jay said

I should tell you. You can't lose a single operative. FrostNight is coming."

"He didn't say anything else about it?"

I shook my head.

The Old Man scared me. I mean, yes, he was me, but he was a me who had seen so much. I wondered how he had lost his eye. Then I wondered if I really wanted to know.

"Can you send me home?" I asked.

He nodded without speaking. Then he said, "We can. Yes. It'd be an effort. And it'd mean we'd failed. We'd need to wipe your memories, to remove all information about this place; and we'd need to destroy all your world-Walking abilities. But, yes, we could do it. They might wonder where you'd got to, but time doesn't flow at a constant rate across the worlds; you've probably not been gone more than five minutes, so far. . . ." He must have seen the hope on my face. "But would you desert us like that?"

"Mister, no offense, but I don't even know you. What makes you think I want to join your organization?"

"Well, you come with the highest recommendation. Jay said so. Like he said, we can't afford to lose a single operative."

"I—*I'm* the replacement he was talking about?"

"I'm afraid so."

"But I got him killed."

"All the more reason to make it up here. Losing Jay was a

tragedy. Losing both of you would be a disaster."

"I see. . . ." I thought about home—my real home, not these countless different shadows of it. "So you could send me back?"

"Yes. If you flunk out of here, we may have to."

If I closed my eyes, I could still see Jay, looking up at me from the red earth before he died. I sighed. "I'm in," I said. "Not for you. For Jay."

He held out his hand. I reached out my hand to shake it, but instead he enveloped my hand in his huge, hard hand and stared into my eyes. "Repeat after me," he said, "I, Joseph Harker . . ."

"Uh—'I, Joseph Harker . . .'"

"Understanding that there must be balance in all things, hereby declare that I shall do all in my power to defend and protect the Altiverse from those who would harm it or bend it to their will. That I will do everything I can to support and stand for InterWorld and the values it embodies."

I repeated it, as best I could. He helped me when I stumbled.

"Good," he said. "I hope that Jay's faith in you is justified. You'll need to pick up your gear from the quartermaster on duty. The stores are in that square building across the parade ground. It's eleven hundred hours now—enough time to get settled in your barracks and unpacked by eleven forty-five. Lunch is at twelve hundred hours.

Twelve forty you start basic training."

He got up and prepared to go out. I had one question left to ask him.

"Sir? Do *you* blame me for Jay's death?"

His LED eye glittered a cold blue. "Hmm? Yes, of course I do. And so do five hundred other people on this base. You have a hell of a lot to make up here, boy." And he walked out.

It was like being a new kid in a school you hated. Only worse. It was like being a new kid in a school you hated that was run by the army on vaguely sadistic principles, where everyone was from a different country and they had just one thing in common.

They all hated you.

It could have been worse. No one spat in my food, no one dragged me off behind the barracks to beat the hell out of me, no one put my head into the toilet and flushed it. But no one spoke to me, unless they had to. They wouldn't help me. If I was going the wrong way to class, no one would mention it; and when they saw me jogging around the parade ground, sweating and breathless, because I'd turned up five minutes late . . . well, that was the only time I'd see my fellow recruits smile when they looked in my direction.

If I was accidentally knocked over in rope climbing; if I got the weakest gravity repulsor disk in disk riding; if I got the oldest, grubbiest, most underpowered wand in Magic 101; if I ate at a table on my own, in the middle of a crowded mess hall . . . well, that was what happened.

I didn't mind.

No, more than that: I was glad. They weren't punishing me any more than I felt I ought to be punished. Jay had saved my life; he'd rescued me from that ship in the middle of the Nowhere-at-All; he'd saved me from my own stupidity more than once. And I'd paid him back by getting him killed.

So everybody got in line to hate me, and I was right at the front of the line.

A spray of sleet hit me in the face, and I clipped the cup back to my belt and I turned back to the rock face. "Okay," I said. "Time to head back up."

Jo said nothing. She flapped her wings to shake off the icy water and turned back to the rock face. She climbed, and, after a few minutes, so did I.

I was shivering. It was easier now, though: Jo seemed to have an instinct for the handholds and footholds, and I followed her. Which went fine until the rain grew harder.

I looked up. The rock that Jo was standing on was crumbling beneath her foot.

"Hey!" I yelled, frantically signaling her to move.

But she ignored me. Then the rock gave way, and Jo

slipped back down in a shower of pebbles. She fell directly onto me, knocking both of us down the cliff face.

It was a long way down, and we were tumbling fast together.

I grabbed her by the waist and pushed away from the cliff with my legs. She got the idea at once and flapped hard with her wings. Maybe she couldn't keep both of us up for long, but we didn't need to be up for long.

She landed back on the ledge where I'd eaten my soup.

"I tried to tell you," I told her.

"Yeah," she said. "I knew you were trying to get my attention. I just wasn't going to look at you."

I stood in the rain and shivered. "How did you know Jay?" I asked her.

"The same way all of us did. One day we started Walking. He came and got us and brought us back here. Mostly he got us out of trouble on the way."

"Well, that's how he found me. And he saved my life on the way, three or four times. And he gave up his own life getting me here. But I don't think he would have treated me like this. And I don't think he would have let me treat myself like this."

There was a pause. Then she looked me straight in the eyes, with brown eyes that were like looking into a mirror. "You're right. I don't think he would either. I'll spread the word."

We climbed back to the top of the cliff in silence then, but it was an okay silence.

After that, things got better. Not much better. And not all the way. But they improved.

CHAPTER TEN

And I'd thought Mr. Dimas's tests were hard.

Exams on InterWorld would make a Mensa chapter gulp with disbelief. It would have smoke coming out of the ears of our best brain trusts. How do you answer a question like: "Is the improbability factor of a time-reversed world solipsistic or phenomenological?" Or: "Describe six uses for the anti-element pandemonium." Or how about: "Explicate the gnosis available from Qlippothic Beings of the Seventh Order."

Try wrestling with stuff like *that* when you barely passed Home Ec.

I'd been at InterWorld's boot camp for about twenty weeks now. Twenty weeks of round-the-clock exercises, classes in martial arts I'd never heard of (one of our instructors was from a world where Japan had united with Indochina to produce, among other things, fighting styles that made Tae Kwon Do look like drawing room dancing), survival skills, diplomacy, applied magic, applied science and a host of other things not likely to be found in the curricula of most high schools—or M.I.T., for that matter.

After twenty weeks of InterWorld food and intensive exercise, intensive study—heck, intensive everything—I was as lean as a stick of beef jerky and was working toward the kind of musculature and reflexes I'd seen advertised in the back of old comic books and had always dreamed of sending away for. I also had a head full of facts, customs and other esoterica that would allow me (theoretically) to pass as a native on a good number of the Earths where humanity looked like me.

Of course, my newfound skills at subterfuge and blending in wouldn't do me much good on some of the other Earths we knew about, such as the one Jakon Haarkanen hailed from. Jakon looked like an example of what might happen if there was a wolf in the family tree maybe thirty thousand years back. She was sleek and feral and weighed about eighty pounds, most of it lean, sinewy muscle covered with short dark fur. She was a real practical joker—she liked to crouch on one of the rafters in the dormitory's upstairs hall and then surprise you as you walked underneath by dropping down and knocking you to the floor. She had sharp teeth and bright green eyes, and she still looked kind of like me.

As you can maybe tell by the description, Jakon was one of my more distant cousins.

At the moment she and I, along with Josef Hokun and Jerzy Harhkar, were standing on one of the higher balconies of Base Town, taking a rare break from studies and watching a herd of antelope creatures thundering along a narrow river valley beneath us. It was noonish, and the ward fields had been relaxed enough to let the planet's fresh cooling breezes blow through. I stood next to an Iigiri tree, weighted with clusters of orange-red berries. Before us were flower beds full of royal lilies, honeybush, jove blossoms and blue lotus. There were cycads, conifers and flowers that hadn't existed on most Earths for millions of years. Their combined scents were enough to make me dizzy, especially after the dry filtered air below levels.

Base Town, like the three or four other domed floating cities across which the forces of InterWorld were spread, had no fixed locale—instead it floated, by a combination of magic and science, across the face of a world where humans were still finding tasty fleas on each other. It was like living in a perpetual tour of a planet-sized national park, vista after vista of spectacular natural beauty. We skimmed the top of forests that spanned half a continent, hung over a waterfall that would never bear the name Niagara, safely sat ringside and watched volcanic eruptions, tornadoes, floods. . . .

There were worse places to go to school.

We were moving east and about due for another phase shift. It happened right on schedule; as we watched, the world before us flickered, then seemed to melt away, flowing into a momentary glimpse of the In-Between's psychotic landscape before we came back to reality. After the aurora faded we were floating over a barren tundra with the sun high overhead. I could see a herd of aurochs stampeding away and a handful of lugubrious mastodons methodically stripping a large willow tree. The air was colder, and I saw, in the distance, the twinkling cliffs of mountainous glaciers as they crept toward us, shining like icebergs in the sun.

Same valley. Different world.

We do tend to surprise the locals when we enter; that's why we stick to prehistoric time lines. Less chance of discovery. It was all part of the security measures that InterWorld took to keep the Binary and HEX from finding them. The floating domed cities shifted at random among a cluster of several thousand Earths about halfway down from the Arc's center. That's why, even with my skills in Walking the In-Between, I needed help to find the particular world Base Town was on.

The help had come in the form of that strange little equation that Jay had drawn in the bloody sand. Like most of InterWorld's stuff, it worked by a combination of magic and science.

$$\{IW\}:=\Omega/\infty$$

wasn't a mathematical argument, exactly, nor was it entirely a magical spell. It was a paradox equation, like the square root of minus one; a combinatorial abstract, a scientific statement created by magical means.

$$\{IW\}:=\Omega/\infty$$

was a memetic talisman that each of us carried in our heads and nowhere else, and which allowed us to "home in" through the last few layers of reality to reach Base Town, wherever it was. It was a key, and you needed to be a Walker to work the lock. Flying ships powered by bottled undead Walker energy couldn't do it; nor could spaceships cruising through the video Static of underspace, powered by deep-frozen 99 percent dead Walkers. You had to be a real live Walker carrying the key in your head for it to work, which made it virtually impossible for either of the empires to find InterWorld.

That was the theory, anyway.

All of which explained the sense of security that allowed us to feel comfortable being out in the open while the four of us quizzed one another for tomorrow's exams: *Basic Theories of Multiphasic Asymmetry in Polarized Reality Planes* and *The Law of the Indeterminate Trapezoid as Observed in the Ceremony of the Nine Angles.*

Even after five months, the majority of the recruits were still pretty cold toward me. They didn't leave me alone at my table in the mess hall anymore, but they weren't exactly running to sit next to me; and while they spoke to me, and were civil, there was still a sense of reserve there I couldn't ignore. I was one of them—I *was* them, and you can't keep hating yourself. But you still don't have to like yourself all the time. So if I was never going to be Mr. Popular, well, I'd learned to deal with it. The three alternate versions of myself—the term our lecturer in Levels of Reality 101 used was "para-incarnations"—who were with me up on the deck were the closest I had to friends—which put them pretty much in the category of "not enemies."

"Okay," I was saying, "list the attributes that remain constant from plane to plane."

"Um," said Josef, and he scratched his nose. "All of them?"

"There are only four, Josef."

Josef was from an Earth more dense than mine, which meant a higher gravitational field. Josef was built like a two-legged tank, and was probably stronger than any human being has a right to be. He explained it to me once—something about longer, wider tendon attachments, increased striated/smooth muscle ratio, and greater bone density. All I know is he was twice my height and almost strong enough to reach around behind and pick himself up by the seat of his pants.

"Symmetry, chirality, correspondence and, um."

He looked like he could maybe beat a golem at a game of checkers, if somebody blindfolded the golem first. But as a matter of fact he was pretty smart—had to be, to keep up with all the other Joeys.

"Give up?"

"It's not laterality, is it?" he asked without much enthusiasm.

"Yes," I said. "It is."

"My turn," said Jerzy to me. "What are subliminal isorithms, and how do they apply to Walkers?"

"I know this one," I said. "Wait, don't tell me . . ."

Jerzy grinned. "Don't worry—I won't."

Jerzy looked much closer to me on the evolutionary highway. The main difference between humanity on Jerzy's world and on mine was that Jerzy's people had feathers instead of hair. Oh—and the women gave birth to eggs instead of babies. That's probably related. It was always startling to see Jerzy coming around a corner—he had pretty much my face, a bit sharper maybe in the nose and cheekbone department, but his eyebrows were soft gray down and his "hair" consisted of colorful featherlike growths about eight inches long. The tips were bright scarlet. Jerzy was a very bright, quick, acerbic guy. He was probably the closest thing to a real friend I had in a few million Earths.

"An isorithm is something to do with how high things are, and subliminal isorithms are what allow Walkers to walk from one world to another without winding up twenty-five feet under the ground. It's what keeps us at ground level wherever we go."

He made a face. "Well, yes," he said. "Sort of. But you'll have to get closer to the wording here. Hey, did you see that, up there?"

"Where?" I hadn't seen anything.

"Up there. High in the sky. It looked like . . . I don't know. It looked like a bubble or something. No, it's gone now."

I stared up into the blue sky but saw nothing at all.

The last week had been all exams, which meant late-night cramming in addition to all the physical training during the day. The delta wave programming we got during the three or four (if we were lucky) hours of sleep we were averaging helped, but you had to supplement that with old-fashioned hitting the books if you wanted that extra edge. I'd never worked so hard—it felt like my brain was on fire. I'd wake up in the night muttering "Perpetual motion and the philosopher's stone," and "It's a chthonic entity" or "under-space (aka the Static) and the Nowhere-at-All are merely facets of perception at ninety degrees to each other." I was studying too hard. The others weren't having it any easier.

Then, to make matters worse, I started having problems with J/O HrKr. J/O is pretty much me: I mean, he looks like me. A head smaller than me—the same height I was when I was his age. Same nose. Same freckles, even. He looked like he was around eleven and was younger than me—than most of us—and maybe that irritated him. Or part of him. He was, after all, half computer. Or, as he called it, "bionanotic enti-ties." Where he came from, they all were.

"Makes sense," he told me one day, when we were doing a session in the Hazard Zone. "After all, you wear a wristwatch. So why shouldn't I have the same information available as a retinal readout?"

I took a dive, rolled and tumbled to avoid a cluster of writhing steel cables that suddenly erupted from the floor where I stood. The cables arced toward J/O, spreading out to envelope him. J/O raised his right arm, which was covered with a layer of mesh. There was a blinding ruby light, a sound like bacon sizzling in a pan; and when my vision cleared there was nothing left of the cables but blackened stumps and the smell of ozone.

"You can wear a sundial on your head for all I care," I told him, doing a backflip to avoid a gout of flame that jetted out of the wall. "I just don't think it's fair that you get to microimage the text books and put them into ROM, when we have to memorize them."

"Your loss, flesh face," he told me. "I got the best system: silicone and molecular spin engineering instead of proteins and nucleotides and nerve connections. Wave of the future, baby."

Jerk. He acted as if he'd invented this stuff, instead of just coming, as he did, from a culture where they start injecting you with computers and machines the size of water molecules at birth. J/O's Earth wasn't a Binary satellite—yet—but it was much further advanced than the Earth I came from.

Once the exams were done—and, no, we never got to know the results, which to this day still hacks me off—we were called into the briefing room, all one hundred and ten of us juniors, and I got to see the Old Man for the first time since I took the oath in the infirmary.

He looked older.

"Welcome, ladies and gentlemen," he said to us. "You are now all ready to begin to take part in the great struggle.

"New worlds are always being created. Some are worlds in which science holds sway"—I saw J/O hold his head up proudly—"others are worlds in which magic is the motive power. Most worlds are mixtures of the two. We of InterWorld have no problem with either ideology. Our problem is with HEX and with the Binary, who both seek to impose their belief systems and methods of reality on other worlds—sometimes through war, sometimes more subtly.

"InterWorld exists to maintain the balance. We are a guerrilla group, outnumbered and outgunned in every way. We could never directly confront either side, for we can never win. Nor do we want to win. But we can be the sugar in the gas tank, the chewing gum on the seat and the nail for want of which the kingdom was lost.

"We protect the Altiverse. We maintain a balance. That is our brief—to stem the twin tides of magic and science, to insure a mixture of both wherever we can.

"You recruits have graduated from step one of basic training, and you all have my congratulations. Well done. Tomorrow you will be split up into small teams, which will be sent on training missions. In each case, this will be just like a real field operation, except that, obviously, you will not be in any real danger. You will be visiting friendly or neutral Earths, and you will have an objective which will be attainable, if not actually easy to attain, in the time period given. You will have twenty-four hours to complete your mission and return to base.

"Each team will consist of four recruits and one more experienced operative, just in case things go wrong. Which, I hasten to add, they will not. . . ."

In the mess hall afterward, I sat with Jerzy.

"Ever get homesick?" I asked him.

"Why would I be homesick?" he asked, puzzled. "If I were not here, I would not be back in my family's nest: I would be dead. I owe InterWorld my life."

"Point taken," I said, feeling envious—I was homesick all the time, sometimes to the point of actual pit-of-the-stomach pain that blipped my biosensors and puzzled the medics. I wouldn't admit it, of course. I changed the subject. "I wonder if we're going to be on the same team on this training exercise."

"Why ponder and cogitate in a futile manner," said a soft voice from behind us, "when, simply by perambulating to the bulletin board at the hindmost of the hall, full and utter discovery of all the facts may be yours." Jai bowed his head and smiled and passed by.

"Did he say that the team assignments are already posted?" Jerzy asked me.

"I think so," I said, and we raced each other through the hall to get to the bulletin board, which was already crowded with recruits copying down relevant information onto notepads and shouting out things like "Wah! I'm with Joliette! Better bring the garlic," and "Hey, Jijoo. We're on the same team tomorrow!"

Jerzy threw back his head and crowed. "I'm with the Old Man's team!" he shouted. For the Old Man himself was actually taking out a group of four recruits. I was envious but also a little relieved that it wasn't me: The Old Man still scared me sometimes. J/O was with the Old Man's team, too. So was J'r'ohoho. He's a centaur, and he let us know in no uncertain terms last week that if he hears any more "eats like a horse" lines during mess we'll all be wearing horseshoe facial imprints. I figured the Old Man had taken the most promising candidates for his own team. I wasn't surprised he hadn't taken me, and I couldn't blame him.

My team's experienced operative was Jai, enigmatic and, as he once described himself, sesquipedalian. "Means he uses lots of long words," said J/O, who has access to several dictionaries in his head.

There was me. There was Josef, big as a bull. There was winged Jo, who hadn't spoken to me since that day on the rocks, but who didn't actively ignore me either. And there was Jakon, the wolf girl. There were worse groups I could have been picked for.

Then the bell went off, and off we trooped to Practical Thaumaturgy, with lab.

The alarm went off half an hour before dawn, waking me from an uneasy dream in which my family and I had, for some dream reason, packed up and moved into the In-Between. I alternated between trying to climb the hall stairs, which had turned into an M. C. Escher etching, and listening to a lecture from Mom about how bad grades could get me eaten by demons. Mom had gone Picasso, with both eyes on one side of her nose, Jenny had turned into a wolf girl and the squid was a real squid, who lived in a cave under the sea. I was actually glad to get out of bed.

We lined up for porridge, except for the carnivorous versions of me, who had ground auroch meat, cooked or, in Jakon's case, raw. Then we picked up our stores and assembled on the parade ground in groups of five.

Several groups were given the okay to leave, and they stepped into the In-Between and were gone.

Then the Old Man's assistant ran out of his office and called him over. They were standing pretty near us. I heard "They can't? Now? Well, it can't be helped. When Upstairs calls, after all. Tell them I'll be there."

He turned to Jai. "You can carry an extra individual, can't you?"

Jai nodded. He was holding the sealed orders which would take us on our training mission.

The Old Man went back to his group and told them the news. Then he pointed to various places in the parade ground.

My spirits rose; I hoped that Jerzy would be assigned to our group.

Instead J/O sauntered over. "Hey, new team," he said. "Well, I'm ready to go. We who are about to die, and all that."

"Do not say that, even in jest," said Jai. He tapped me on the shoulder: I would be the team's Walker. "Commence our intradimensional excursion."

"What?" Jo asked.

Jai smiled. "Take us out of here," he said.

I took a deep breath, opened a door into madness with my mind, and, in single file, we marched into it.

The In-Between was cold, and it tasted like vanilla and woodsmoke as I Walked.

CHAPTER ELEVEN

I'd been back in the In-Between several times since that first horrifying jaunt; basic training stuff, honing my ability to find various entry and exit points, learning what surfaces not to step on (the big mauve disks that sailed along like car-sized Frisbees seem to be easy transportation, but put a foot on one and it'll suck you down like hungry quicksand) and how to recognize mudluffs and other dangers. I still didn't like the place. It was too bizarre, too unstable. In one of the many survival classes we took, the instructor described navigating the In-Between as "intuitively imposing directional order in an inchoate fractal hyperfold." I said it struck me more like trying to find your way out from inside a giant Lava lamp. She said it came to the same thing.

But, believe it or not, there were ways to get through it and come out where you wanted to be. None of them were easy—especially not for someone like me who had difficulty getting to the store on a two-dimensional grid like Earth's surface. No one was really sure how many dimensions were embodied in the In-Between, but InterWorld's best brains had determined that there were at least twelve, and possibly another five or six rolled up in various subatomic nooks and crannies. It was full of hyperboloids, Möbius strips, Klein bottles . . . what they called non-Euclidean shapes. You felt like you were trapped inside Einstein's worst nightmares. Getting around wasn't a matter of looking at a compass and saying "This way!"; there weren't just four directions, or eight or even sixteen. There were an infinite number of ways one could go—and it took focus and concentration, like finding the hidden Indians in a picture of the forest. More than that, it took imagination.

Once we came through the portal (it looked like a department store revolving door this time, only with dripping stained glass in the panels) we stood on one facet of a giant dodecahedron while Jai opened the sealed orders. He pulled out the paper inside and dropped the envelope (it promptly sprouted wings and flew away; littering is hard to do in the In-Between). He opened the instruction sheet, scanned it silently, then said, "We are to proceed to the following coordinates," and read them out. "It's one of the neutral worlds of the Lorimare confederation. And there we will retrieve three beacons that will have been placed within a square mile of our exit point."

I took the paper and looked at it. There were things you could tell about your destination just from the coordinates. If you think of the Arc—what we called the Altiverse—as a bow, thick in the middle and thinning toward the edges, then this particular Earth was pretty much in the middle of the Arc's curve, at the thickest part. The worlds on the outer parts of the horns were either solidly magic or solidly techno, but the demarcation grew fuzzy and overlapping as you got near the center. Out on the horns, Binary and HEX ruled millions of Earths with no challenge or ambiguity, but as you drew closer to the middle from one side or the other their iron grasps relaxed a little. There were Earths where one or the other of the two ruled from behind the scenes, using fronts like the Illuminati or the Technocrats. And there were worlds whose civilizations were based on science or sorcery but had not yet been assimilated by either of our enemies. My Earth was one of those—a little farther along the science curve than the magic. The world we were going to was even closer to the center of the Arc—its scale of civilization had been tipped early on toward science, but it could just as easily have gone the other way, toward magic.

Jai pointed to me and said, "Please escort us to our veridical destination, Walker."

I nodded, fixed the coordinates in my head and let them pull me this way and that, a psychic dowsing rod. I zeroed in on the particular exit node I wanted—a pulsating plaid torus on the far side of what looked like a field of undulating tofu strips. We jumped, one by one, from the dodecahedron to a huge cypress knee floating in a soft golden glow. I was ready to take them from there to the torus, when suddenly something zoomed past my head, leaving a multicolored streak behind it.

"Mudluff!" Jakon shouted. "Take cover!" Being Jakon, she ignored her own order and dropped into a wolf crouch and growled menacingly, scanning the chaos.

Jo, Jai and Josef followed suit. J/O crouched, raising his laser arm and tracking with his grid eye, trying to get a bead on the threat. He reacted in astonishment when I jumped into his line of fire. "Hold it!" I shouted. "Don't shoot! He's my friend!"

The others looked at me in astonishment. "It's a mudluff!" Jai said, eschewing obfuscation, given the state of emergency. "They're all dangerous!"

J/O tried to maneuver around me to get a clean shot at Hue. I shifted in counterpoint with him, while Hue peered anxiously over my shoulder. "He's the In-Betweener I told you about," I said. "The one who—" I stopped, realizing almost too late that it was unwise to bring up what had happened to Jay. "Who—saved my life," I finished somewhat awkwardly. "Trust me—he won't hurt any of you."

My comrades looked extremely dubious, but they slowly emerged from their various hiding places. Hue prudently stayed behind me. I spoke soothingly to him, hoping to encourage him a bit. "Hey, Hue, how you doin'? It's good to see you again. C'mon out and meet the gang." Things like that. He got a little bolder, but he still stayed within a foot of me. His color scheme pulsed with anxious colors, mostly purples with ripples of turquoise.

"Look," I told them, "we're almost at the portal. Hue's not going to come out of the In-Between." I didn't mention that Jay and I had first met him on a fringe world, one that had some In-Between characteristics but was, on the whole, much closer to normal reality. I was hoping Hue wouldn't— or couldn't—leave the In-Between completely. He was a mudluff, after all, a multidimensional life-form, which meant that he probably couldn't comfortably compress down to the four dimensions of the terrestrial planes. It would be like trying to stuff a giant octopus into a shoe box. At least I hoped so.

"Very well," Jai said reluctantly. He and the others gathered next to me, though none of them wanted to get particularly close to Hue.

"Where do we go from here?" Josef asked.

"Through there." I pointed at the tartan doughnut. Jai leaped forward and dived feetfirst through it. One by one the others followed, until I was the only one left in the In-Between.

I turned to Hue. The bubble creature hovered beside me, undulating with hopeful shades of blue and green.

"Sorry, little guy, but I got business in the real world. Maybe we'll see you on the way back." Although frankly I doubted it. What were the odds, after all, of running into him again in the unknowable, unmappable immensity of the In-Between? Virtually zero . . .

Which meant he had tracked me somehow.

I felt both touched and apprehensive at the thought. I'd never read anything in my studies that indicated mudluffs could sense out people and find them, much less become fond of them—but since the aggregate of what we knew about them would rattle around in a flu germ's navel, that wasn't surprising.

Still, I felt kindly toward the little guy. I found myself hoping he'd stay behind and wait for us.

"Bye, Hue," I said. I dropped through the doughnut . . .

And slid through a portal that shrank down to a pinprick and vanished behind me. Just before it did, however, a tiny, dense soap bubble squeezed out. It quickly expanded to Hue size and fell toward me.

I didn't notice him at first because, as sometimes still happened, my stomach had led the rest of my viscera in an attempted mutiny that took me a minute or so to quell. Then my inner ears negotiated a separate treaty and I was able to stand, albeit a bit shakily, and look around.

I noticed the expressions on my teammates' faces an instant before I saw Hue. "You said he wouldn't come out of the In-Between," Jo said accusingly.

I shrugged as Hue took up what was becoming his customary position just behind my left shoulder. "What can I say? I don't know how to get rid of him. If anyone has any suggestions, I'm open to them."

Nobody did. Jai decided that it was probably better to concentrate on the task at hand, which was finding the first beacon. I started to caution Hue to mind his p's and q's, but let the words die as I looked around us.

It was an impressive sight. We were on a rooftop looking out over a cityscape that resembled nothing so much as the cover of an old science fiction pulp magazine. Tall slender towers, graceful as mosques, rose in Manhattanesque majesty all around us, connected by sweeping ramps and glassine tubes. Air cars—shiny two-person teardrop shapes—flitted from landing platforms through the clean air.

None of us could spend much time admiring the view, though—this world didn't look particularly dangerous, but neither does a coral snake, banded with vivid enamel colors, until it bites you. A rounded kiosk made of gleaming metal and graced with Art Deco vanes stood about three feet away. A sign on it said it was a "lift shaft"—this Earth used a recognizable form of English, thank God. The sliding door was locked, though there was no sign of a locking mechanism.

"Allow me," J/O said. He pointed his arm laser at the intersection of door and kiosk. "Watch me blast this baby out."

"Are you terminally unsociable?" asked Jai. "We are guests in this locality. Wanton destruction of personal property would be nothing more than causeless vandalism." He closed his eyes and touched the door, which slid open. There was no sign of an elevator. But there were metal rungs set into the wall on the far side, and, one by one, we began to climb down, floor by floor by floor, J/O grumbling that he was never allowed to use his laser arm. Hue stayed with us, hovering above our heads. He drifted too close to Jakon once, and her warning wolf growl made him skitter back up the shaft a good twenty feet. I found myself wondering how anything so defenseless had ever survived in the In-Between.

While we descended, Jai took out a device the size and shape of a thimble and held it in his hand. After a moment, it began to float in the air. A tiny LED twinkled on it, and then a pattern of blinks, pointing straight ahead.

"Locator activated," he said. "Object of acquisition resides on the antepenultimate story of this residence."

"Would it kill you to cut back on a few syllables every time you make an announcement?" Jo asked him, her wing feathers fluffing with irritation.

"Yeah," J/O said. "I've got the latest Merriam-Webster chip—twenty teras' worth of dictionaries, thesauri, syllabi, you name it, cross-indexed over sixty reality planes, and some of your lines are still coming up 'no sale.'"

Jai merely smiled. "What good is a vocabulary that isn't used?"

The door opened then, and, one by one, we stepped out

into a laboratory that was so gleaming and polished and high-tech that it would have made Dr. Frankenstein weep with envy. As with the city itself, this place looked like it had started in the 1950s and then skipped over several decades to land squarely in the late twenty-first century. Banks of lights mounted on the high ceiling illuminated everything in a crisp glare. Gleaming banks of computers, their front panels holding huge reels of magnetic tape, lined one wall. There were capacitors, electrode terminals that occasionally crackled with power, ponderous refrigeration units and other pieces of equipment that I didn't recognize.

Oddly enough, though much of the equipment was up and running, there were no people present. Jakon pointed this out. Jai shrugged. "All the more good fortune for us." He aimed his finger around the room, following the thimble's twinkling light pattern until it narrowed to a straight line.

"Up there." He pointed.

"Up there" was a series of shelves maybe twenty feet up, about two-thirds of the way from the ceiling.

"I'll get it," said Jo. She stepped forward, spread her wings—carefully avoiding the crackling current of a Van de Graaff generator—and lifted off. She rose gently upward on those angelic five-foot spans of white feathers, and, watching her, I found myself thinking that the Earth she came from must look like the closest thing to Heaven in the Altiverse.

Jo stopped, hovered near the shelf and reached in behind some articles. Hue seemed fascinated by her ability to fly, but his curiosity was tempered with caution, so he just floated a few feet away and watched. Jo pulled out a small gizmo that seemed to be blinking, though you couldn't be sure—the flashes seemed almost to be in the ultraviolet, right on the high end of visible light. It was disturbing in some low-key way, and so I looked away, peering past a control console and monitor screen to look through a window.

Something was bothering me, but I couldn't quite put my finger on it. . . .

The lab was three stories down from the top of the tower, and through the window you could see most of the city. I heard the rustle of Jo's wings as she landed behind me, and that faintly disturbing feeling that was stirring around in the back of my head started moving a bit more energetically as she handed the beacon to Jai.

"One down, two to go," Jakon said—or rather, half said and half growled.

"There's got to be more to the test than this," Josef rumbled. He sounded disappointed.

And I wanted to say, *There is, there is . . . Don't let your guard down . . .* but I wasn't sure *why* I wanted to say it. And then I saw one of those sleek little airships swoop by the window, and I knew.

But then it was too late.

I spun around and faced the others, managed to say "It's a trap!" But that was all, because then everything—

changed.

It was like watching a ripple that started in the beacon Jo held—a ripple that spread outward in all directions, washing over everything in its path—including us. I felt nothing except a momentary coldness and disorientation. None of my teammates seemed to be affected either.

But everything else was. That ever-expanding ripple turned into a transparent wave that passed over the equipment and scientific paraphernalia, transforming everything as it went. That merciless fluorescent glare gave way to the flickering yellow light of tapers. A long-range surveillance monitor screen wavered and changed into a crystal ball. A rack of chemicals and solutions held in glass retorts and test tubes became an oaken cabinet housing earthen pots and vials full of various powders, salts and elixirs. A radiation and toxic materials containment chamber became a circle of gold bricks inlaid in the floor and stamped with protective cabalistic signs. The wave—actually an expanding bubble, with us at its center—accelerated as it grew larger, and within seconds the futuristic laboratory had been transformed into a sorcerer's sanctum.

And it didn't stop there. Looking out the window, I could see the wave spreading across the city in all directions like the radiating blast front of a nuclear bomb. The Art Deco skyscrapers and spires rippled, wavered, became Gothic towers of mortared stone. The aerial ramps and tubes vanished, while the darting airships metamorphosed into winged dragonlike creatures who carried human passengers on their backs.

In a matter of a minute or less, the gleaming science fiction city had been turned into a medieval town complete with a castle at its center, with us in its tallest tower. Even the window I was watching through was now an unglazed opening with crosshatching iron bars. Everything had changed.

No, I thought then—*not changed*. You couldn't change what had always been, and this had always been a world ruled by magic, not science. My subconscious had realized that when Jo had flown up to get the beacon. Her wings were far too small to support her purely in terms of lift and air pressure. Jo's people had evolved on a world where magic was in the very air they flew in, and she could fly only when such transmundane power was present.

Like here.

"Back to the roof!" I shouted, and turned toward the elevator shaft, only to find instead a narrow enclosed stairwell, crowded with guards holding spears, swords and crossbows pointed at us.

I called myself six different kinds of a moron. No wonder there had been no people visible save for the far-off ones flying the airships. No wonder the whole city had looked so spic-and-span. A glamour had been laid over the whole shebang, just for our benefit—a spell of seeing that mesmerized the eyes and brain into visualizing and experiencing a false front. Our taking the first beacon—probably a talisman disguised as the beacon—had triggered the spell's dissolution and signaled HEX that we were safely in the net.

No wonder everything had been so easy!

Hue hovered anxiously over me and my companions as the armed guards stepped apart to make way for two people I hoped I'd never see again—Scarabus, the original Illustrated Man, and Neville, that walking, talking, glutinous, life-sized version of the Visible Man model kit I'd gotten once for Christmas. They came down the stairs and stopped, each flanking the stairwell entrance. They seemed to be waiting for someone, and I had no trouble guessing who it was.

There was a rustle of silken robes, and a cloaked figure materialized from the darkness within the stairwell tower. She stepped into the wavering light of the sconces, threw back her hood and surveyed us. Her gaze stopped on me and she smiled.

"Well met again, Joey Harker," said the Lady Indigo. "What a pleasant surprise. And look! This time you've brought your friends."

CHAPTER TWELVE

"Get behind me!" shouted Jai, proving again that he could say exactly what he meant when he had to.

He was floating about six inches above the floor. He raised both hands, and something like a huge translucent umbrella took shape in front of us. Jai's psychokinetic abilities depended neither on magic nor on science, he told me once, although they were stronger on magical worlds. They were, he said, *spiritual*. Whatever. I just hoped that they could keep Lady Indigo at bay.

A shower of crossbow bolts struck the umbrella shield, slowed in the air and fell to the floor, drained of all forward movement.

Lady Indigo gestured, and a bead of vermilion fire hung above her palm. She put it up to her lips and blew. It hurtled toward Jai's umbrella shield. When it hit the shield, it exploded into a sort of syrupy crimson flame. Jai looked like he was gritting his teeth. He began to sweat and then, slowly, to tremble. The effort of holding the shield in place was taking its toll on him.

Then there was a *pop!* and the shield vanished in a blaze of crimson fire. Jai collapsed to the floor.

I heard snarling. Josef had picked up Jakon, the wolf girl, and threw her, almost bowled her, up the stairwell. It was like one of the games we'd play back on Prime Base, but this one was for real. She knocked a dozen archers down as she rolled like a gymnast. Then she sprang from the stairs down onto Neville. I think she expected to knock him to the floor, but she hit his jelly flesh, and she froze, like someone paralyzed by a jellyfish's sting. He picked her up like a child's toy, shook her once violently and dropped her. She didn't move again.

Josef grunted and charged Neville. It must have been like being charged by a tank, but it barely seemed to faze the jelly man. Josef plunged his fist deeply into Neville's vast stomach, which simply distended like something in slow motion without apparently troubling Neville at all.

The jelly man laughed, a vast, muddy, bubbling laugh. "They send children against us!" he said. Then he held his hands out: The jelly flesh shot forward, covering Josef's face. I could see him struggling to breathe, his eyes distended. Then he collapsed as well.

Jo fluttered upward until she was in the rafters of the room. She was up in the top corner, out of range of the arrows.

Lady Indigo snapped her fingers, and Scarabus knelt at her feet. She touched one of her fingers to a picture that writhed its way up his spine. It was a picture of a dragon.

And then Scarabus was gone, and in his place, huge and hissing, was a dragon, complete with wings and clawed limbs on a nightmarish pythonlike body. It flew up and wound itself around the rafters, moving at blinding speed toward Jo. She fluttered back against the wall, terrified.

Almost lazily it looped around her, then it slammed her against the wall and retreated to the floor, carrying her unconscious body with it.

When it was curled back on the floor again it shook itself, and once more it was Scarabus. Jo lay on the floor beside him.

It became very quiet.

I wanted to do something, but what could I do? I had no special abilities or powers, like the others, and I wasn't carrying any weapons; none us were, except J/O, whose weapons were built-in. It was only a training mission, after all.

"What sweet friends you have," said Lady Indigo. "And all of them are Walkers, too, of a kind. None of them as powerful or able a Walker as you, but when cooked down and bottled they'll each power a ship or two. Eh?"

Now all this took a while to tell, but it merely took a handful of seconds to occur. So now it was just me and J/O. I may have had my problems with the little brat—I guess I was a brat, too, when I was his age, but right now it was him and me—and Hue, who had shrunk to the size of a bowling ball and turned a terrified shade of translucent gray.

"I don't think so," J/O said in response to Lady Indigo's question. He aimed his laser arm at her. There was a gentle ruby glow at the tip but nothing else. I decided this wasn't the time to point out that technology won't work beyond a certain point in a solidly magic world.

J/O said a word that he must have gotten from one of his dictionary programs, because he didn't get it from me.

And then Lady Indigo said a word herself that you wouldn't have found in any dictionary, and she moved her hand just so, and J/O stood very still. He had a goofy expression on his face.

"Take them to the dungeon," she told the soldiers. "Each of them should be prisoned in a different cell. And chain them down." She walked over to J/O. "Go with these nice men to the cell they'll have ready for you and help them chain you up. I'll come and see you when you're all settled in."

He looked up at her like a spaniel looking at God. It made me feel sick, because I knew that must have been what I'd looked like back when Jay rescued me from the pirate ship.

You know what made me feel sickest, though? I'll tell you. It was this: They'd left me for last, because they didn't care about me. Everyone else was a problem to be solved or a nuisance to be batted away. I was a triviality. I wasn't important.

"What about me?" I asked.

"Ah yes. Little Joey Harker." She walked over to me. A little too close. I could smell her perfume, which seemed to be a sort of mixture of roses and rot. "What perfect timing. I was hoping to catch a top-class Walker in our little snare, but you are more than I could have hoped for. You're needed back at HEX. Very urgently. There's a big push just about to start. And you—you could power a *fleet* of battleships. There's a courier schooner leaving in an hour, and you'll be on it. You'll be paralyzed, of course. Scarabus?"

The tattooed man nodded. "It's all ready, my lady."

"Good," she said. And she flung some kind of spell at me.

I suppose it must have been the paralysis spell, but I couldn't say for sure. Because before it reached me, Hue bobbed down and intercepted it, and the spell hit him with a spray of golden sparkles and evaporated into nothing.

Hue turned the exact color of the fluffy pink towels in Lady Indigo's bathroom. I wondered if it was some kind of mudluff joke.

Lady Indigo was not amused. She looked at her henchmen. "What *is* that creature? Neville?"

"Never seen one before," said the jelly man. He threw a large green canopic jar at Hue. It hesitated when it touched Hue's surface, frozen for a moment in space and time, and then it vanished completely. Green and gold and pink swirled around Hue's translucent soap-bubble skin, and then it went a solid white.

Hue hung there bobbing gently in space for a moment. It seemed to be looking at the people in the room, trying to decide what to do next.

And then it swooped down toward me.

For a moment, I was touching Hue's surface, cold and slippery and, strangely, not disgusting—and then the world exploded.

I saw a lot of things at once, as if they were superimposed over one another: I saw Lady Indigo and the cellar; I saw the scientific glamour world; I saw my fallen teammates—only I could see them all from every angle, up and down and sideways and inside out. And it was as if I could see them through time, as well—all the intersections that put them into this place.

And from there I slipped into a world that made utter sense. It was in focus and sane and entirely logical. And I knew, on some level, that this was now the In-Between. But it was the In-Between from the point of view of a multidimensional life-form. It was the place the way that Hue saw it.

Our minds were touching. And I started to have a tiny, growing sense of what Hue actually was . . .

. . . and . . .

I fell to what passes for the ground in the In-Between. In this case it was a gentle film of copper spray which seemed to be held together by surface tension. A flock of tiny incongruent whorls devolved across the heavens.

The place made no sense anymore, which was an enormous relief to me. Hue was hanging solicitously in the air beside me. Or maybe a Hue the size of Vermont was a thousand miles away from me, glowing a warm and reassuring shade of blue. It extruded a pseudopod and gently spread it into a fan of finger shapes, moved them in a regretful arc and then absorbed them back into the bubble body.

"Thanks for getting me out of there," I said. "But I have to get them back again. They were my team."

If a featureless colored bubble can shrug, Hue shrugged.

I concentrated on the world-gate coordinates . . .

. . . and nothing happened. It was as if that world no longer existed. As if the coordinates were meaningless.

I concentrated harder. Nothing happened.

"Hue, where *were* we? What happened back there?" Hue seemed to have lost interest in me. He spun around, bobbed into a patch of fuzzy wind-chime music and vanished.

"Hue! Hue!" I called, but it was no use. The mudluff had gone.

I tried one last time to reach the world I'd taken my team to, but with no results.

And then, with heavy heart, I thought

$$\{IW\}:=\Omega/\infty$$

and I made my way back to base, to try and get some reinforcements, to try and get my team out of Lady Indigo's clutches.

Base was crowded with returning milk-run teams, carrying their beacons in triumph. I saw J'r'ohoho the centaur stumble past, with a boy who could have been me on his back.

I ran over to the first officer I saw and told her my story. She paled, called someone over, and they conferred.

Then she took me down to the room behind the stores, which was the nearest thing Base had to a jail cell. She pulled something that looked a lot like a standard Earth-issue gun and told me to sit down on the plastic lawn chair that was the only item of furniture in there, while she stood by the door with her gun trained on me.

"Try to Walk, and I'll blow your head off," she told me, in a no-nonsense sort of way.

What made it worse was that somewhere in the infinitude of possible worlds, in a stony dungeon beneath a castle moat, my team was chained up, and hurt, and abandoned.

CHAPTER THIRTEEN

They came and asked me questions, and I answered them as best I could. It was a bit like a debriefing and a bit more like an interrogation.

There were three of them. Two men, one woman. All of them me but older.

And they asked the same questions over and over. "Where did you take them?" "How did you escape?" and, over and over, "Where are they?"

And I told them. How I thought I took the team to the right place. How Hue, the little mudluff, pulled me out of there. How I tried to move back and find them and couldn't get there.

"You know that we've already sent an independent rescue team into that world. It's just a regular techno world, like a hundred thousand others. They say your team never arrived there. They've never seen you."

"Maybe we didn't go there. I know it felt like the place I was given coordinates for. It seemed like a techno world, and then it—changed. And they got us. But I didn't do it on purpose. I swear I didn't!"

They asked me questions for hours, and then they left, locking the door behind them.

I couldn't figure out why they locked the door. I could have Walked out—the InterWorld planets have potential portals everywhere. Maybe it was symbolic. Either way, there was nowhere I wanted to go.

The door was opened the next morning, and I was led out, blinking at the light that came through the dome.

They took me to the Old Man's office. I'd been there only once before. His desk takes up most of the room, and it's covered with stacks of paper and folders. No computers or scrying spheres that I could see, but that didn't mean they weren't there.

The Old Man looks to be in his fifties, but he's much older than that, even in linear time. He's seen his share of action, and more; despite cell reconstruction, he's pretty banged up. His left eye is a technoconstruct. Lights flicker inside it, green and violet and blue. There're all kinds of legends about what it can do: shoot laser beams and transfiguration spells, read your innermost thoughts, see through walls—you name it. Maybe it can do all those things; maybe none of them. All I know is that when he looks at you, you want to confess every wrong thing you've ever done and throw in a bunch you haven't for good measure.

"Hello, Joey," said the Old Man.

"I didn't do it on purpose. I didn't mean to get us lost, sir. Really I didn't. And I tried to get back there."

"I hope you didn't do it on purpose," he said quietly. He paused. "You know . . . some people here had doubts about taking you on as a trainee Walker after Jay's death. I told them that you were young and untried and impetuous but that you had the potential to be one of the best. And that, on some level, as he had wished, you were replacing Jay. One for one.

"But it's turned into one for six . . . and, well, the cost is too high. You took them to the wrong place. You lost them. And it looks like you ran out on them to save your neck."

"I know what it looks like. But that didn't happen. Look, I can find them—just let me try."

"No." He shook his head. "I'm afraid not. We'll call it a day here. You won't graduate. Instead, we're going to take your memories of this place away. We're going to take your memories of everything that's happened since you left your own Earth. And we're going to remove your ability to Walk."

"Forever?" It couldn't have sounded worse if he'd said they were taking my eyes.

"I'm afraid so. Look, we don't want you to get hurt. If you start to Walk, you'll be a beacon. You could lead them straight to your world—or back to InterWorld.

"So we're sending you back to your Earth. We won't even

adjust the temporal differential. It'll work in your favor—
you won't have been gone too long."

I tried to think of something to say in my own defense,
but all I could think of was "But I *did* take them to the coordinates I was given. I know I did. And I didn't run out on
them." And I'd said that the day before, to too many people,
too many times.

Instead I asked, "When are you going to take my memories?"

He gave me a look of great pity, then. "It's already done,"
he told me.

I looked up at the strange man with the mismatched eyes
in puzzlement. "Who . . . ?" I said. Something like that.

"I'm sorry." he said. And then everything went dark.

"Amnesia's a funny thing," said the doctor. It was my family M.D., Dr. Witherspoon. He had delivered the squid, and he treated Jenny when she had the chicken pox, and he stitched up my leg last year after I was dumb enough to go over Grand River Falls in a barrel. "I mean, in your case, you've lost about thirty-six hours. If you aren't faking it."

"I'm not," I told him.

"I don't believe you are. I tell you, the whole town went crazy searching for you. I don't think that even Dimas is going to be able to keep his job after *that* nonsense. Sending you kids out into the city and telling you to find your own way back . . . well." He peered at my eyes, shone lights into them. "I can't find any evidence of concussion. Don't you remember *anything* before you walked into the police station?"

"Last thing I remember," I told him, "is getting lost with Rowena. And after that it all goes weird, like trying to remember a dream."

He looked at his clipboard and pursed his lips. The bedside telephone beeped, and he answered it. "Yes," he said. "He seems fine. . . . My dear woman, he's a teenage boy. They're practically indestructible. Don't worry. Sure, come and pick him up in an hour or so." He put the phone down. "That was your mother," he told me. He made a note on my chart.

"Well," he said then, "maybe your memory will come

back. And maybe you'll have thirty-six hours of your life lost forever. No way to tell right now.

"You're looking leaner then I remember you," he added. "Is there anything worrying you? Anything you need to talk about?"

"I keep thinking I lost something," I said. "But I don't know what."

Some people thought I was faking. I heard one story in school about how I'd hitchhiked all the way to Chicago, which was kind of disturbing—I mean, for all I know I might have hitchhiked to Chicago. Or gone even farther.

They did a segment on the local eleven o'clock news, with interviews with Mayor Haenkle, and the chief of police and with an old guy who demonstrated with models that I'd been taken off in a flying saucer.

Dimas didn't lose his job. It turned out that each of the cards he'd given us before we set off had had a tracker chip built into it. So he knew where each of us had been all the time.

Except for me, of course. My little red blip had gone from the screen on his laptop (he was cruising around in his Jeep, making sure none of us got on buses or called home for rides). And it never turned up again. That was one of the things that the saucer guy pointed to as evidence that I had been taken into space.

Ted Russell thought it was hilarious. He started calling me "saucer boy" and "space captain" and "Obi-Wan Harker" and things like that whenever he saw me. I did my best to ignore him.

I grew kind of popular, but it was the way a bear in a cage would have been popular. Some kids wanted to be my new best friends, and some stared and pointed from across the lunchroom.

Rowena Danvers came up to me after math, later that first week. "So, where did you go that day?" she asked. "Was it a flying saucer? Or did you go to Chicago? Or what?"

"I don't know," I told her.

"You can tell me. I was the one who waited for you on that stupid street corner for half an hour, after all. I won't tell anyone."

"I don't know," I told her. "I wish I did."

Her eyes flashed angrily. "Fine, if that's how you feel. I thought we were friends. You don't have to trust me if you don't want to. I don't care about you anyway." And she stomped away, and all I could think was *I know what you'd look like with your hair cut really, really short.* And then I wondered why I'd thought that.

One day—it was a couple of days after the local news piece aired—Ted Russell went too far. I think he hated all the attention I was getting. Or maybe he was just as mean as a skunk with a toothache, and he hadn't done anything nasty recently.

Either way, between periods, he came over to me from behind and took me by surprise, knuckling me hard in the kidney.

It all happened kind of fast, then.

I dropped my center of gravity by bending my legs slightly, took a step back and slid my other foot over into a modified cat stance (and don't ask me how I knew it was called that). I grabbed his wrist, bent it in one of the few ways wrists were not designed to bend, pulled him over and brought the edge of my other hand down on the back of his neck. In just over a second Ted had gone from causing me pain to writhing on the ground in agony at my feet. I shut off the autopilot that had taken over just in time to keep from performing the last movement in the sequence, which I knew (again, don't ask me how), would have resulted in a very dead Ted.

He got to his feet and stared at me as if I'd sprouted green tentacles. Then he ran from the room, which was good, as I was completely frozen. I didn't know what I'd done. I didn't know how I'd done it. It was as if the muscles had known what to do and didn't need me.

I was just glad that no one else had seen it.

Things went on like that for about two weeks.

"You ought to be kidnapped by aliens more often," said my dad one evening over dinner.

"Why?"

"Straight A's, for the first time in human memory. I'm impressed."

"Oh." Somehow it didn't seem that cool. Schoolwork was pretty simple now: It was as if I knew how hard it could be and what I was capable of doing. I felt like a Porsche that had learned it wasn't a bicycle anymore but was still taking part in bicycle races.

"What does 'Oh' mean?" Mom picked up on that immediately.

"Well." I gestured with a stalk of broccoli. If you wave it around enough, sometimes they don't notice you're not eating it. "It's just math and English and Spanish and stuff. It's not like it's hyperdimensional geometry or something."

"Not like it's *what*?"

I thought about what I'd just said. "Dunno. Sorry."

Most of the time I forgot about my thirty-six-hour loss. But when I fell asleep at night and, sometimes, when I woke up in the morning, I could feel it at the back of my head. It itched. It tickled. It pricked and it tingled. I felt like I was missing a limb in my head; as if an eye that had opened had closed forever.

I was fine, unless I was lying in the dark. And then it *really* hurt. I'd lost something huge and important. I just didn't know what.

• • •

"Joey?" said Mom. Then she said, "You're getting too big to be Joey. I suppose you'll be Joe, soon."

My upper arms shivered with goose pimples. It was there, again. Whatever it was. "Yeah, Mom?"

"Could you take care of your brother for a few hours? Your father and I are going to visit my gemstone supplier. There's a semiprecious stone from Finland I've never heard of he says would be perfect for me."

Did I mention my mom designs and makes jewelry? It was a kind of hobby that got a bit out of control, and it had paid for the extension on the house.

"Sure," I said. The squid is a cool little kid. He's actually kind of fun for an eighteen-month-old. He doesn't whine (much) and he doesn't cry unless he's tired, and he doesn't follow me around too much. And he always seems pleased when I play with him.

I went up to his room in the annex. Every time I walked up those stairs I found myself wondering if the nursery was going to still be there this time.

It's like those weird paranoid thoughts that go through your head when there's not enough going on, like when you're in the bus on the way home from school and you wonder if maybe your parents moved away without telling you. You must have had them, too. I can't be the only one.

"Hey, squidly," I said. "I'm going to be looking after you for a couple of hours. You got anything you want to do?"

"Bubbles," he said. Only he said it more like "Bub-bells."

"Squid, it's the beginning of December. Nobody blows bubbles in this weather."

"Bub-bells," said the squid sadly. His real name is Kevin. He looked so dejected.

"Will you wear a coat?" I asked. "And your mittens?"

"Okay," he said. So I went down to the kitchen and made a bucket of bubble mixture, using liquid dish-washing soap, a jigger of glycerin and a dash of cooking oil. Then we put our coats on and went into the yard.

The squid has a couple of giant plastic bubble-blowing wands, most of which he hadn't used since September, which meant that I had to find them, and then I had to wash them, as they were caked with mud. By the time we were ready to start blowing bubbles, it was snowing gently, big flakes that spun down from the gray sky.

"Hee," said the squid. "Bub-bells. Ho."

So I dipped the bubble wand into the bucket, and I waved it in the air; and huge multicolored soap bubbles came out from the plastic circle and floated off into the air; and the squid made happy noises which weren't quite words and weren't quite not; and the snowflakes touched the bubbles and popped the little ones, and sometimes the flakes landed on the bigger bubbles and slid down the sides of them; and every soap bubble as it floated away made me think of . . .

. . . *something* . . .

It was driving me crazy that I couldn't quite tell what.

And then the squid laughed and pointed at a bobbing bubble and said, "Hyoo!"

"You're right," I said. "It does look like Hue." And it did. They'd taken everything from my head, but they couldn't take Hue. That balloon looked just like the . . .

. . . just like the mudluff that was . . .

" . . . *It's a multidimensional life-form* . . ."

I could hear his voice saying it, under that swimming, finger-painted sky . . .

Jay.

I remembered him, lying bloody on the red earth after the monster attacked. . . .

And then it came back. It all came back, hard and fast, while I was standing out in the snow with my baby brother, blowing bubbles.

I remembered it. I remembered it *all.*

PART III

CHAPTER FOURTEEN

I could Walk again.

Don't ask me how. Maybe there was a glitch in whatever brain-scrubbing gizmo they used on me. Maybe Hue was some kind of unanticipated variable they hadn't programmed (or deprogrammed) for. . . . Whatever. All I know is, standing there in our backyard, shivering in that light dusting of snow, watching my little brother happily chasing those bubbles around, a series of firecrackers was going off in my head, each one illuminating a memory that hadn't been there before.

I remembered everything: the grueling days and nights of study and exercise; the infinite diversity of my classmates, all variations on a theme that was Joey Harker; the tiny supernovae going off apparently at random in the Old Man's artificial eye; the seething Technicolor madness that was the In-Between . . .

And the milk-run mission that had gone wrong, being captured once again by Lady Indigo and my rescue—mine and only mine—by Hue.

I stood there, shivering from a chill that had nothing to do with the weather, mechanically dipping that bubble wand into the soapy solution and creating bubbles, and wondered what I should do now.

I remembered the shame and helplessness I felt when I came back without my teammates. What had happened to them? What had Lady Indigo and Lord Dogknife done with them? *To* them? I desperately wanted to find out. And I knew I could. I knew I could Walk again, could go back through the In-Between. The formula for finding Base Town burned clear and bright in my mind. I could get there, oh yeah.

But did I want to go?

If I left my Earth again, I could *never* come back. Every time I opened a portal it was like sending up a signal flare to HEX and the Binary. I would be taking a chance of luring the bad guys here. Each Walker, I'd been told, had a unique psychic signature that could be traced. I guessed that the Binary had thousands of sequenced mainframes on the lookout for my configuration, just as HEX kept a phalanx of sorcerers on twenty-four-hour duty for the same reason. I couldn't put my family and my friends in that kind of danger.

If I never Walked again, the chances were trillions to one against either side ever deciding to conquer this particular world. It was virtually certain that I could grow up, get married, have kids, get old and die without ever having to hear about the Altiverse again.

But to never Walk again . . .

I don't know if I've mentioned yet that Walking is like any skill you're good at, in that I enjoyed it. It felt good, it felt *right*, to use my mind to open the In-Between, to pass from world to world to world. Chess masters don't play for money, or even for competition—they play for love of the game. Mathematical savants don't get their kicks from gardening—they juggle set theories in their heads or daydream pi to umpty-ump places. Like a trained gymnast, now that I remembered my ability, I itched to use it.

I could not imagine living a lifetime without ever Walking again.

But neither could I imagine it without ever seeing Mom or Dad, or Jenny or the squid again. I had signed up once, but that had been done mostly out of guilt over Jay's death—I hadn't realized what I was getting myself into.

This time I knew all too well.

I'd been mustered out once—they wouldn't let me off that easily a second time. If I showed up at Base Town again, they would most probably court-martial me. Oh, they might have a different name for it, but a firing squad by any other name is still a bunch of guys with rifles pointed at you. I didn't know if I'd ask for a blindfold or not, and had no great desire to find out.

But if I stayed here, I'd have to live with the knowledge that I'd left people I cared for in trouble while I got away.

I wished those damned soap bubbles hadn't sparked whatever circuit held these memories. Ignorance might not have been bliss, but at least it wasn't the stew of regret I found myself in now.

The snowfall had turned to a cold rain. I could have told myself that it was the source of the water running down my cheeks, but it doesn't rain warm salt water. And I'd lied to myself enough.

I watched one soap bubble that Kevin was chasing. It was floating higher than the others, about level with the garage roof. It drifted into the bare branches of the nearby oak, and I expected to see it vanish in a soundless pop.

It didn't.

Instead, it hovered there for a moment, then drifted slowly toward me. The squid ran along underneath it, yelling in frustrated futility because he couldn't reach it. The bubble moved along against the slight breeze that had come up, and stopped and hovered in front of me.

"Hi, Hue," I said.

The mudluff rippled orange with pleasure, then shot up over my head, passing above the roof. I turned, craning my neck to follow him, but he was already gone.

"Bub-bell?" Kevin asked plaintively. "Bub-bell? Hyoo?"

I nodded. "That's right, squid kid." I looked down at him, watched him wipe his nose on his coat sleeve and said, "Time to go in."

I stayed up most of the night, worrying at the problem from first one end and then the other. I couldn't talk to Mom or Dad—they're great parents, but both of them together couldn't summon up enough imagination to deal with one extra Joey, never mind an infinity of them. Who else could I talk to? Certainly not my classmates. My guidance counselor had been found sobbing quietly in his office last semester, and hadn't been replaced yet. Most of my teachers were one-trick ponies; after five months under the whip at Base Town I already knew more than any of them ever could know or handle knowing. Out of the entire teaching staff there was only one person who might possibly listen to me and not call for the men in white coats.

Mr. Dimas leaned back in his chair and stared at the acoustic tiles above him. He had a vaguely stunned expression, and I couldn't really blame him—after all, the story I'd just told him probably wasn't one he'd heard before.

After a minute he looked at me. "When we started talking," he said mildly, "you asked me to consider what you were going to tell me as purely hypothetical. I assume that's still the case?"

"Uh, yes, sir." I had thought that maybe telling him the story with an unnamed imaginary friend at center stage instead of yours truly might make it a little easier to swallow. "This, uh, friend of mine—he's really kind of between Scylla and Charybdis." He shot me a penetrating look, and I realized I had used an expression that I'd learned at Base Town instead of here. "So, anyway," I hastened on, "what do you think he should do?"

Dimas got his pipe going before speaking. When he did finally speak, it was to ask a question. "So, according to the instructors at Base Town, the universe only spins off doppelganger worlds when *important* decisions are made, is that right?"

"Uh, basically. Only it can be real hard to tell right away what's important and what's not. I mean, they say a butterfly flapping its wings in Bombay might start a tornado in Texas. If you were to step on that butterfly before it had a chance to fly—"

He nodded. Then he looked at me and said, "I know this will sound strange, but do me a favor, Joe." Most people had taken to calling me Joe lately; I'm not sure why. It took some getting used to. "Sure, Mr. Dimas," I said.

"Take off your shirt."

I blinked, then shrugged. I wasn't sure where he was going with this, but—and this was kind of sad in a way—I also knew that he was no match for me in any kind of fight, fair or unfair.

So I took off my jacket and the loose T-shirt I wore under it. Mr. Dimas looked at me without comment for a moment, then gestured that I should put them back on.

"You've gotten quite a bit leaner," he observed. "More muscular, too—as much as someone your age can, which isn't all that much—you're still genetically programmed to grow taller rather than bigger."

I decided the best thing to do was keep quiet and wait. I hoped he'd answer my question eventually.

He did. "As far as your hypothetical friend goes, I agree with you—it's a tough decision all around. But if we get down to basics, it seems to me that the question your friend has to answer is: Does one person's happiness—or even one person's life—outweigh the fate of countless worlds?"

"But I—that is, *he* doesn't know for sure that'll happen!"

"*He* knows the possibility exists. Don't get me wrong—I sympathize with the pain of his decision. And some men look nice with beards." He read the question in my face and said, "So they don't ever have to face themselves in the mirror when they shave."

I nodded. I knew what he was saying, and I knew he was right. It made it clearer what had to be done. Not easier, no, not by any means. But clearer.

I stood up. "Mr. Dimas, you're a hell of a teacher."

"Thank you. The school board doesn't always agree, but

they have used the words 'Jack Dimas' and 'hell' in the same sentence. Quite often."

I smiled and turned to go.

He asked, "Should I expect to see you in class tomorrow morning?"

I hesitated, then I shook my head.

"I thought not. Good luck, Joey. Good luck to all of you."

I was going to say something smart, but I couldn't think of anything smart to say, so I just shook his hand and got out of there as fast as I could.

I sat down on the edge of the bed and handed my old Star Blasters plastic armor and ray gun—both sets—to the squid. The ray gun fired an infrared beam that a sensor on the chest plate picked up and registered—if you did it right.

He was thrilled—he'd always wanted the kit. "Jo-ee! Tinkoo!" He was way too young for them, but he'd grow into them.

In a way, I told myself, I'd be helping make sure of that.

I told Jenny she could have my CD and DVD collection, for what it was worth. She and I had pretty much the same tastes in movies—basically, anything that ends with the Death Star or a reasonable equivalent blowing up real good was okay by us. The music was problematical, but what she didn't like she could either sell or grow into.

She was pretty suspicious of this sudden generosity, of

course. I told her I had to go visit some remoter branches of our family, and I wasn't sure when I'd be back. I didn't add "if ever." Maybe I should have, but if you think it's easy saying good-bye to your younger siblings, maybe forever—well, it's not.

Mom and Dad were harder still. I couldn't just tell them I was leaving home, maybe forever—on the other hand, I wanted them to know somehow that I would be okay (even though I wasn't 100 percent sure of that part myself).

I made a pretty big mess of it, all told. I told them I was joining "something like" the army. Dad said I don't think so, and that all he had to do was make a few phone calls to keep *that* from happening, young man. Mom mostly cried and asked where she had failed as a parent.

I guess it shouldn't have surprised me that I would screw it up—after all, I didn't exactly have a stellar record to date in taking care of people close to me. It ended with me promising not to "do anything rash" tonight, and we would "discuss it further in the morning."

But I couldn't wait until the morning. I had to do it quickly, while my gumption was up, as Granddad used to say. I stayed awake until two A.M., long after everyone else had gone to sleep—then I got dressed and headed downstairs.

Mom was waiting for me.

She was sitting in the armchair by the cold fireplace, wrapped in her bathrobe. At first I had the horrible feeling that I'd sleepWalked somehow and slipped into another parallel Earth, because Mom was smoking, and she'd quit that a good five years ago.

I was frozen, caught there in the light of the living room lamp like a rabbit in a car's headlights. She looked at me, and there was no anger in her eyes—just a kind of resignation. Which was, of course, ten times worse than anger would have been.

At last she smiled, and it didn't reach her eyes, and she said, "What kind of a mom would I be if I couldn't read you after all this time? Did you think I wouldn't know that you were leaving? Or that if I kept on sleeping I'd miss my chance to say good-bye?"

A thousand replies went through my head, some truthful, some lies, mostly a combination of the two. At last I said, "Mom—it would take too long to explain, and you wouldn't believe any of—"

"Try me," she said. "Just tell me. Tell me everything. But tell me the truth."

And I did. I told her everything that I could think of. I told her the whole thing, from the beginning to the end. And she sat there and smoked and coughed and looked faintly sick (and I didn't know if that last was because she hadn't smoked in so long or because of what I was telling her).

Then I got to the end, and we sat silently in the room.

"Coffee?" said my mother.

"I can't stand the stuff," I told her. "You know that."

"You'll grow into it," she said. "I did."

She got up and walked over to the percolator, and poured herself a cup of coffee.

"You know what makes it worse," she said suddenly, urgently, as if we had been arguing about something and now she was coming back with the kicker, "what makes it worse isn't worrying about whether or not you've gone crazy or you're lying to me or any of that nonsense. Because you aren't lying to me. I mean, I've known you for a very long time, Joey. I know what you do when you lie. You're not lying." She took a swig of her coffee. "And you aren't crazy. I've known crazy people. And you aren't one of them."

She pulled another cigarette out of the pack, but, instead of lighting it, she began to take it apart while she talked, peeling off the paper, pulling out the tobacco, inch by inch, stripping it down to paper and tobacco and filter, all in a neat pile in the ashtray.

"So, my little boy is going to war. Obviously I'm not the first mother in history this has happened to. And from what you're saying, I'm not even the first—the first *me* this has happened to. But what makes it worse is that from the moment that you walk through that door, you're dead to me. Because you're never coming back. Because if you . . . if you get killed, rescuing your friends or fighting the enemy or in your In-Between World . . . I'll never know.

"The Spartan mothers used to say, 'Come back with your shield or on it.' But you're on your way, and I'll never see you again, shield or no shield. No one's ever going to send me a medal or a—what do they do, now that they don't send telegrams?—or a message, saying 'Dear Mrs. Harker, we regret to inform you that Joey died like a . . . died like a . . .'"

I thought she was going to cry, but she took a deep breath and just sat there for a bit.

"You're letting me go?" I asked.

She shrugged. "I spent my life hoping I would have kids who would be able to tell the difference between right and wrong. Who, when the decisions, the big decisions, need to be made, would do the right thing. I believe you, Joey. And you're doing the right thing. How could I ever stop you now?

"Wherever you go. Whatever happens to you. Know this, Joey. I love you, I'll always love you, and I think . . . I *know* you're doing the right thing. It just . . . hurts, that's all."

Then she hugged me. My face was wet, and I don't know if they were her tears or my own.

"We'll never see each other again, will we?" asked my mom.

I shook my head.

"Here," she said. "I made it for you. It's a good-bye thing.

I'm not sure what else I can give you." And she pulled a little stone on a chain from her pocket. It looked black and then, when it caught the light, it glinted blue and green like a starling's wing. She fastened it about my neck.

"Thanks," I said. "It's lovely." And then I said, "I'll miss you."

"I couldn't sleep," she said. "It gave me something to do." And then she said, "I'll miss you, too. Come back, if you can. When you've saved the universe."

I nodded. "Will you tell Dad?" I asked. "Tell him I love him. And that he's been the best dad anyone could hope for."

She nodded. "I'll tell him. I could wake him up, if you like . . . ?"

I shook my head. "I have to go," I told her.

"I'll wait here," she said. "For a bit. In case you come back."

"I won't," I told her.

"I know you won't," she said. "But I'll wait."

I went out into the night.

It was below freezing outside. I slipped into the mind-set that had supposedly been scoured from my head, and started casting about for a potential portal.

I hoped there would be one nearby—I didn't like the notion of having to walk (without a capital W) very far in this weather. I can't just open a portal to the In-Between anywhere I feel like. I wish I could. But it doesn't work that way. Certain transdimensional points of space-time have to be congruent, and these come and go. It's like catching a cab—if you're lucky one might stop for you outside your house, but it's more likely you'll have to hike a bit, maybe even as far as the nearest hotel or restaurant where there's a taxi stand. There are places where you're more likely to find potential portals. Unfortunately, they're not always near restaurants or hotels.

It may sound strange, but I didn't let myself think about that conversation with Mom. There were just too many surprises to deal with—I could feel the fuses in my mind threatening to blow every time I came close to thinking of it. I concentrated instead on finding a portal.

I didn't feel the faint tingle in my head that usually indicates there's one nearby, so I started trotting down the street, my breathing puffing out in clouds as I went. I found myself wondering what the soap bubbles I'd been blowing earlier for the squid would do in subzero weather.

A moment later I found out—sort of.

Hue came swooping out of the night and hovered before me. He pulsed an urgent spectrum at me: green, orange, yellow, pearl. It occurred to me that maybe his patterning was even more complex than I had assumed it was—that instead of being a symptom of basic emotional states it was actually a language. Because he certainly seemed to be trying to tell me something now.

When he was sure he had my attention, he scooted off, pausing now and then to make sure I was following. Which I was. We stopped in a tiny park—practically nothing more than a lawn without a house behind it—about six blocks from my house. Hue seemed to be waiting for me.

I knew what he wanted. I cast about for the nascent portal I knew would be here. And found it.

I looked up at Hue, floating there patiently. "Thanks, buddy," I said. And I fitted my mind into that transdimensional congruency like a key into a lock, and opened that lock and swung the door wide.

Beyond was a shifting, rickety landscape that looked like a *Doctor Strange* comic book. I squared my shoulders, took a last look around, drew a deep breath—

and went for a Walk.

CHAPTER FIFTEEN

Hue was nowhere to be seen when I got into the In-Between, which made me feel kind of relieved, to be honest.

Don't get me wrong; I was grateful to the little guy. But if I'd never met him . . . well, my life would sure have been a heck of a lot simpler. Jay would still be alive, for one thing. And maybe I'd still be happy and at home with my family and not off trying to save the Multiverse, or whatever it was that I was trying to do.

I stood on a rock that felt the way that fresh oregano smells and that tumbled through the madness of the In-Between in a crashing arpeggio of double-bass music. I rode it like a surfer rides a board, and I thought about where I should go from here.

I said I remembered everything, but that wasn't quite true. I remembered *almost* everything. But, rummage around in my head as much as I wanted, I couldn't find the key that would let me go back to Base Town. (There was something . . . some way . . . but it was as elusive as the shape of a hole in your tooth after it had been filled or the name of a man you knew that definitely began with *S*—if it didn't begin with *L* or *V* or *W*. It was gone. Which makes sense, I guess—of all my memories, the key to InterWorld Prime would be the biggest secret to keep.)

Meanwhile, in the back of my head, a voice like gas wheezing through honey was saying, "We are ready to begin the assault on the Lorimare worlds. The phantom gateways we will be creating will make a counterattack or rescue impossible. When they are empowered, the usual Lorimare coordinates will then open notional shadow realms under our control. Now, with another fine Harker at our disposal, we will have all the power we need to send in the fleet. The Imperator of the Lorimare worlds is already one of ours. . . ."

Lord Dogknife's words had meant nothing when I had heard them originally, coming from the mouth of Scarabus—they had just been one more thing among entirely too many things that I didn't understand. But now, in the light of everything that had occurred, they made perfect—and horrifying—sense.

Phantom gateways, leading to notional shadow realms. Yes.

Shadow realms, like the one that six kids, heading out to find three beacons on a training mission, wound up in. We thought we were going to one of the Lorimare worlds, and instead we wound up in a shadow dimension. The concept had been touched on as a theoretical possibility in one of the classes at Base Town: They were also known as "oxbow worlds," named after the oddly shaped lakes that were sometimes left when a meandering river cuts off a section of itself. Think of the river as a time stream and the oxbow lake as a slice of reality that's somehow been pinched off, doomed to run an endless loop of existence, over and over. It might be anywhere from a few seconds to years, even centuries. The point is that it's sealed off from the rest of the Altiverse, no more detectable or accessible than the theoretical universe inside a black hole.

If Lord Dogknife's sorcerers had somehow managed to open a way to one of these shadow dimensions, they could put a seeming spell on it, make it look like whatever they wanted it to—and then drop us out of it and into one of the HEX worlds. Which was exactly what they'd done. There had been no way for us to detect the trick, either by instrumentation or by Walking. The perfect trap.

But, once opened, that shadow realm was no longer inaccessible. I still remembered how to get there.

I couldn't go back to InterWorld. I didn't have that knowledge. Okay, fine.

It didn't mean I couldn't start looking for my friends.

I envisioned the coordinates that had taken us into the trap, and, gently, I nudged them open with my mind.

A huge, egglike door dilated several yards in front of me with a low bitter-chocolate-scented screech.

I didn't go through it. I just watched and waited. After a moment, the door closed once more, and then it shrank to nothing and vanished. Where the door had been, however, was a dark place like a shadow that rippled and flapped like a flag in a thunderstorm.

That was the trapdoor. That was the portal that led to the shadow dimension where they'd taken my team.

That was where I was going.

I Walked toward the shadow door. Before I could enter, however, something was suddenly in the way, bobbing and hanging in space. It was a balloon the size of a large cat, and it was blocking my way.

"Hue," I said.

Bottle green and neon pink flickered across its surface, as if in warning.

"Hue, I have to go through there."

Hue's surface changed, pushed and pulled, and I was looking at something that resembled a balloon caricature of Lady Indigo. Then the image *sproinged* back into a balloon.

"I couldn't get back there before because you were stopping me, weren't you?"

A deep affirmative vermilion.

"Look, I *have* to get back there. They may have died a long time ago, or they may have only been put into chains five minutes ago—you know how screwy time can get when you go from world to world—especially these shadow dimensions. But they were my people. And I took them there. The least I can do is get them out—or die trying."

He contracted, as if he were thinking. Then he drifted upward and out of my way. He looked a little sad.

"But, hey, if you want to come with me—well, a friend is always good to have around."

Hue ran through a set of bright colors I don't think you can see outside of the In-Between and purposefully bounced down to me. He hovered over my left shoulder.

Together we stepped into the shadow.

I was cold then, for a moment, like stepping into a river on a warm day, and then the world shimmered and re-formed.

I was up on the roof, in a world which looked like something out of *The Jetsons*. And then Hue floated in front of my face, forming himself into a kind of large lens. I looked at the world through the huge bubbly mudluff, and saw . . .

. . . a gray sky. Saw that I was standing on the turret of a sad-looking castle. The whole place felt like an empty stage set, no longer in use. I couldn't see anyone anywhere around.

"Okay," I said to Hue. "Let's go find the dungeons."

CHAPTER SIXTEEN

This is how to find dungeons, if you ever have friends in durance vile in a castle somewhere:

Try to keep out of sight. Find the back stairs. Then just keep going down until there isn't any more down to go, to where the corridors are narrow and smell of damp and mildew, and it's dark enough that, without the weird light that goes with you (if you're lucky enough to have a mudluff coming along) you can't see a thing. When you get to that place, I guarantee the dungeons are just around the corner.

The castle was more or less deserted. I ducked out of sight when I heard footsteps at the other end of a corridor, but that was all. And the people going past looked more like movers: They wore white overalls and were carrying chairs and lamps away with them. They looked like they were closing the place down.

I found the dungeons in about twenty minutes, no problem.

Well, one small problem—they were empty.

There were nine cells, nine windowless holes in living rock, with heavy iron doors that were solid save for small barred windows. All of them were empty. The only sounds were the skitter and chitter of rats and the dripping of water on mossy stones. I took a chance and shouted their names: "Jai! Jo! Josef!" But there was no reply.

I sat down on the stones of the dungeon floor. I'm not ashamed to say I had tears in my eyes. Hue *flooped* from around me and bobbed in the air beside me, patches of glow moving across his surface.

I said. "I'm too late, Hue. They're probably all dead by now. Either they got boiled down like the HEX people said, or they died of old age waiting for me to come back. And it was . . ." I was going to say *my fault*, but I wasn't sure that it was, really.

Hue was trying to attract my attention. He was floating in front of my face, extruding little multicolored psuedopods.

"Hue," I said, "you've helped a lot so far. But I think we've come as far as we can now."

An irritated crimson blush crossed the little mudluff's bubble surface.

"Look, " I said. "I've lost them! What are you going to do? Tell me where they are?"

Hue's surface shimmered, and then became whirls and clusters of stars in a night sky above and below. It was a place I recognized. Jay and Lady Indigo had called it the Nowhere-at-All. The Binary people called it the Static. By those or any other names, it was the fringe area of the In-Between, the long route for traveling between the planes.

"Well, even if that's where they are," I said, "there's no way I can follow them there."

But Jay'd followed me, hadn't he? He got me off the *Lacrimae Mundi*.

It could be done, then.

But I didn't know *how* to do it. I could only Walk through the In-Between itself. To reach the Nowhere-at-All would require knowledge of a whole different set of multidimensional coordinates, from someone familiar with those levels of reality—

I looked up. "Hue?" I said.

The mudluff moved away from me, slowly, foot after foot, until he was at the end of the dank corridor. And then he came barreling toward me, faster than a flowerpot falling from a window ledge, and even though I knew what he was going to do, I couldn't help flinching back as he filled my vision and there was a—

poppp!

—and my world imploded into stars.

The mudluff was nowhere to be seen. Instead, everything felt very familiar. I got that déjà vu feeling of *I've been here before*, but of course I hadn't: Last time I was falling through the Nowhere-at-All Jay was falling beside me, and we were falling away from the *Lacrimae Mundi*.

Now the wind between the worlds was whipping at my

face and tearing my eyes; and the stars (or whatever they are, out in the Nowhere-at-All) were blurring past; and I was flailing, terrified at the emptiness of nothing but more terrified still because now I wasn't falling away from anything.

I was falling *toward* something.

Imagine a doughnut or an inner tube—your basic toroidal shape. Paint it with something black and kind of slimy. Now take five of these and twist and turn and meld them together like those balloon thingies street artists sometimes do for kids—although I think that if you made one that looked like this for a kid, he'd start crying and not stop. Still with me? Now make the whole thing the size of a supertanker. Last, cover every curving surface of what you now have, which is a big black tubular evil *thing*, with derricks and towers and machicolated walls and ballistae and cannons and gargoyles and . . .

Get the idea?

This was not something you wanted to be falling toward. Trust me. It was something you wanted to be falling *away* from, as fast as possible.

But I didn't have a choice.

I squinted my eyes against the wind. There were two or three dozen smaller ships—galleons, like the *Lacrimae Mundi*, and ships smaller and faster than her—arranged around the big black thing. They looked like ducks escorting a whale.

I knew I was looking at Lord Dogknife's attack armada and dreadnought. It was the only thing it could be. They were beginning the assault on the Lorimare worlds.

I had finally found where my friends were being held prisoner—assuming they hadn't already been reduced to Walker soup. The problem was that in a minute or so I was going to hit it like a melon dropped from a skyscraper, and there wasn't a single thing I could do about it. The Nowhere-at-All isn't outer space. It has air and something like gravity. If I hit the ship, I was dead. If I missed—and I had about as much chance of that as an ant missing a football field—I'd keep falling forever, unless I could open a portal into the In-Between, and there was no guarantee of that. I'd only made it last time because Jay was with me.

What would Jay do? I asked myself.

I thought you'd never ask, said a voice in the back of my head. It sounded like my voice, only a decade older and infinitely wiser. It wasn't Jay or his ghost or anything like that. It was just me, I guess, finding a voice that I'd listen to.

You're in a Magic region, now, Jay's voice continued. *Newtonian physics are more of a suggestion than a hard-and-fast rule. It's strength of will that's important.*

It was a rehash of the lectures from Practical Thaumaturgy, or what we called "Magic 101." "'Magic' is simply a way of talking to the universe in words that it cannot ignore," our instructor had told us, quoting someone whose name I've already forgotten. "Some parts of the Altiverse listen—those are the Magic worlds. Some don't and would rather that you listened to them. Those are the Science worlds. Understand that, and the whole thing is kind of simple."

Of course, "kind of simple" is a relative concept in a school where even the remedial classes would give both Stephen Hawking and Merlin the Magician nosebleeds. Still, I had learned enough to know that the place I was in now was a place of raw and unfocused magic. A "subspace" that worked more by the rules of a collective consciousness than by mechanistic principles.

Will. That was the key.

You got it, said Jay in the back of my head. *Now bring it home.*

That giant evil woven doughnut thing was increasing in size as I fell toward it. It didn't look particularly soft, and it looked damn hard to miss.

Okay then, I decided. I wouldn't miss it. But I was not falling toward it—I was *rising* gently toward it. Rising so slowly, so gently that when I touched its surface it would be like thistledown touching the grass, a feather landing on a pillow—so delicately as to barely be there at all.

All I had to do was convince this part of the Altiverse that I wasn't tumbling to my doom.

Which meant convincing myself . . .

I'm not falling, I told myself. *I'm rising, easily and lightly. Soft and slow* . . .

And I managed to ignore the tiny, sensible voice in the back of my head that was screaming in fear.

I wasn't falling. I *wasn't* falling. . . .

It seemed like the wind in my face was easing up. Then everything suddenly shifted perspective a hundred and eighty degrees, and while my stomach was still trying to deal with that . . .

I hit the surface of the ship a lot harder than thistledown touching grass—hard enough, in fact, to knock the wind from my lungs and leave me gasping. But nothing was broken. I said thank you to Jay's voice in the back of my head as I lay on the surface of the ship, holding on to a rope, trying to catch my breath.

Eventually I was able to sit up and look around. Hue was nowhere to be seen—hadn't been since he somehow shifted me from the dungeon to the Nowhere-at-All. Okay, I was on my own—and I was on the ship.

Now what?

The answer wasn't long in coming. Suddenly a hand grabbed me by the neck. More hands hauled me to my feet. They forced my arms behind my back and they marched me into a turret and down a dozen narrow stairwells, deep inside the huge dreadnought, to an enormous chamber that looked to be part map room, part inquisition chamber and part high school auditorium.

There was a smell in that room as if something had died some months ago, and they hadn't yet found what it was to take it away—or didn't care. It was a smell of rot and decay and mold.

Lady Indigo and Neville the jelly man were there, along with fifty or more other people I had never seen before. Some of them looked standard human—some were a *lot* more exotic.

And then there was one that I'd never seen before, but I knew who he was the minute he entered. He was the biggest man I had ever seen: so big, and so perfectly proportioned that it seemed as if everyone else in the room were no bigger than a little child. He wore black and crimson robes. His body, what I could see of it, was human and muscled like Michelangelo's *David*. It was flawless.

But his face . . .

How to describe it? If you ever saw him, you'd never be able to forget him. His face would swim up at you as you began to fall asleep, and you'd wake up screaming.

Imagine a man who had started to transform into a hyena, like a werewolf turning into a wolf. Imagine him caught halfway through the transformation: his face half snout, his beard half coarse dog hair, his teeth sharp and made for ripping carrion. He had piglike eyes that gleamed red, with horizontal slits, like a ferret's. A flattened nose and a jaw perpetually twisted into a ghastly parody of a smile.

He reminded me in a distorted way of pictures I'd seen of Anubis, the jackal-headed Egyptian god who conducted the dead to judgment. Maybe that was a better description, since that was pretty much what he was going to be doing to me.

But it wasn't how he looked that promised nightmares. It was the sense of what lay *behind* that horrible mutated face—the knowledge that, to this thing, this monster, those nightmares were sweet entertainment. They were *Mary Poppins*–style Disney dances in the park.

Lord Dogknife smiled at me with sharp, sharp teeth and said, in a voice like honeyed swamp gas, "We were disappointed not to have picked you up in the snare last month, Joseph Harker. Thank you *so* much for returning." He turned his hyena head. "You were right, Lady Indigo. The most powerful Walker in a decade. I can smell it. He'll make fine fuel for the *Malefic*."

He turned back to me, and I nearly screamed as those hideous eyes found me again. "You are fortunate," he told me. "There is no other ship with the facilities to strip you completely of all extraneous matter, to flense you of flesh and hair and bones and fat, to reduce you to your absolute essentials: the power that lets you Walk from world to world, which is the power that lets *us* travel the Nowhere-at-All. No other ship but the *Malefic*.

"Take him away," he said then, and several lackeys

approached me as he said it. They seized me and started to drag me away from Lord Dogknife.

There was a sudden sparkle of colors above my head. I recognized the rainbow swirls, and my heart gave a great leap of relief. Hue had appeared and was bobbing toward me. I hoped he was planning to somehow teleport me out of there, as he'd done before when my team and I had been captured by Lady Indigo.

Lady Indigo said, "The mudluff, my lord." There was no concern in her tone.

"Indeed," Lord Dogknife said calmly in that thick, glottal voice. "I expected as much." He held up one hand, to reveal a small glass pyramid, like a prism. He placed it on the floor and took a step back, muttering a single word as he did so. It sounded like *"smucklethorrup-gobslotch,"* but it probably wasn't. There was a burst of light, black light—not like the purple light that you shine on posters to make the colors glow, but real black, like rays of obsidian, like a flashbulb going off in negative. It enveloped Hue, who began to turn white, and to shrink, and to *change*.

I knew that if Hue could have screamed, he would have done so.

"No!" I screamed—but it didn't matter. The beams of blackness somehow *compressed* the little mudluff, squeezed him in a direction at right angles to all three dimensions in this world. Then the black rays began shining down into the

little prism, and in seconds they were gone, leaving nothing but a white afterimage on the back of my eyes.

Lord Dogknife picked up the prism. Even from where I was standing, I could see a tiny bubble inside it, turning angry reds and furious crimsons. "They told me that the creature had become attached to you, boy," he said. "So I brought along a holding tank for it. We used them, oh, many years ago, when we tried to colonize some of the madness places between the worlds. The creatures were a nuisance. The little tank won't hold it for long—ten, twenty thousand years at the most—but I fancy none of us will be around when it breaks out."

He put the prism into an inner pocket.

"I have often wished," he said to me—and I don't think I can ever really explain how disquieting and horrible it was to have him talking directly to me, looking straight into my eyes. It was bad enough when he addressed the room, but when Lord Dogknife looked at me, I felt like he knew every bad thing I'd ever done. And more than that—that he felt the bad things I'd done were the only bits of me that mattered and that everything else was insignificant and stupid.

"I have often wished," he said again, "that we could harness the mudluffs. If we could use their energy, the way we use Walker energy, we would rule every world and every universe with ease: The whole glorious panoply of creation would be ours. But, alas, it does not seem practicable. There was one such attempt: But where the Earth upon which it was tried once was, now there is nothing but cosmic dust. Nothing larger than a baseball remains of it. No, we must make do with the life essences of children like you." And he winked at me, as if he were telling me some slightly dirty joke. *He* was the thing that smelled like it had died a long time ago, the smell I'd noticed upon entering the huge chamber. You could taste the rottenness under the scent of dust.

I have never, in my life, been so scared of *anything* as I was of him. There may have been a little magic in the fear. But if there was, he didn't need it.

"In your lifetime that is still to come," said Lord Dogknife, "or to put it another way, boy, in the next thirty, forty minutes, you may take comfort in knowing that your essence—your soul, if you like—will, in company with so many of you little Walkers, be powering the ships and the vessels that will allow my people and our culture to gain the preeminence in all things that we so justly deserve. Does that make you happy, boy?"

I didn't say anything.

The yellow fangs spread into a parody of a friendly smile. "I'll tell you what," he said. "Go down on your knees to me now. Kiss my feet. Promise to serve me forever in all things. Then I'll spare your life. We have enough fuel to power the invasion. We brought every bottled soul we could find to this party. What do you say? Kissie footie?" And he waggled one of his huge feet at me. It was covered with black hair, and the toenails were claws.

I knew I was going to die then, because I wouldn't kiss his feet. I looked him in the eyes and said, "You'd kill me anyway, wouldn't you? You just want to humiliate me first."

He laughed, and the room filled with the stench of rank meat, and he pounded on his leg with his hand as if I'd just told the best joke in the world. "I would!" he said, between bursts of laughter. "I *would* kill you anyway!" Then he drew breath. "Ohh," he said, "I needed that. I'm *so* pleased you decided to drop in."

Then: "Take him down to the rendering room," he told those holding me. "Time to resect and reduce him and the others. No need to make it painless." He turned back to me and winked once more and explained conversationally, "We find that a lot of pain inflicted on the Walkers during the whole rendering process actually spurs on their spirits when they're bottled. Gives them something to focus on, perhaps. Well, good-bye, lad," and he reached out a huge hand and pinched my cheek, almost affectionately, like an old uncle.

Then he squeezed, harder, and harder. I promised myself I wouldn't cry out, but the pain became impossible to bear.

I screamed.

He winked at me once more slowly, as if we'd just shared

a joke nobody else in the room had gotten, and he let go of my cheek.

They twisted my arms behind my back and they marched me out of there. I was so relieved to be away from Lord Dogknife that, for a few moments anyway, I barely cared that I was on my way to the rendering room.

Whenever I'd run across the phrase "a fate worse than death" in books, I'd wondered about it. I mean, death is about as bad as it gets, and as final, in the usual run of things, I always thought.

But the idea of being killed and cooked and stripped down to whatever makes me *me*—and then spending the rest of eternity in a bottle being used as some kind of cosmic power pack . . .

It made death look good, you know. It really did.

CHAPTER SEVENTEEN

The corridors got narrower and darker as we descended from level to level. They also got hotter, as if the huge dreadnought were steam driven, which increased my sense of descending into an inferno. From the moment I had entered the *Malefic*, dark and gloomy had been the order of the day, and it only got worse as we went down.

We went down still more narrow stairwells—the "rendering room" had to be on one of the lowest levels of the ship. I was grateful for that. It gave me more time to think. There were two guards ahead of me and two behind. The corridors and stairs were, probably intentionally, like some kind of labyrinth, and I knew that I was hopelessly lost.

But as tight and confining as those corridors were, they were nothing compared to the hamster maze my own mind was running in.

Lord Dogknife had ordered me killed along with "the others." That meant only one thing: My team might still be alive.

And if they were, we still had a ghost of a chance.

Only a ghost, though. Five trapped versions of myself

against who knew how many thousands of HEX troopers, sorcerers, demons . . . frankly, it would be long odds if we were up against just Lord Dogknife and Lady Indigo. Without Hue to help us, we had about as much chance as . . . well, as nothing.

I knew all that. Even so, just the possibility that they might still be alive raised my spirits.

There was something definitely hellish about the lower levels of the *Malefic*. I started to imagine that I could smell sulphur and brimstone on the air. And then the guards in front of me opened a heavy wooden door, bound and bolted with bronze, and pushed me roughly through it, and the smell got worse.

Imagine Hell, the way you've always pictured it since childhood. Now, imagine that the worst torture pit of Hell is in a room barely as big as a high school classroom. Imagine it was designed by someone who had seen too many really cheap old horror movies, the kind they show late at night in black and white. That was the rendering room.

The rendering room was windowless, just like nine-tenths of the rest of the rooms I'd seen. On the walls hung various tools and implements, scary and sharp and huge. I didn't study them too closely, but they looked like they were to help "cook us down" once we were in the pot and had been boiling for a while. At the back of the room, sitting on a raised grill, was an honest-to-goodness cooking pot, forged of bronze and easily ten feet across, like a giant's cauldron or a cartoon cannibal pot, raised high on three thin metal legs. Some kind of liquid was boiling inside it—from the smell, most definitely not water. It smelled like liquid sulphur, and ammonia, and preserving fluids. There was blood in there, too, I think—the kind of magic they did on that ship draws a lot of power from blood. The fire underneath was being fed with various salts and powders. It burned now green, now red, now blue as different chemicals were added. The smoke and fumes clouded the air and stung my eyes and hurt my lungs. There was a little creature, who looked a bit like a toad and a bit like a dwarf, feeding the fire with the powders, being careful to make sure that only one small handful of powder went on the flames at a time.

None of the people doing the tending and preparation were human. It was kind of hard to make out details, since most of the light in that place came from the flames under the pot, but they had tentacles and feelers. I didn't know if they came from fringe worlds way out on the Arc or if they were people transformed into things that didn't mind the thick chemical smoke or the burning air or the things they had to do down there. I don't suppose it matters. My guards, on the other hand, minded the smoke and the air a lot. Two of them stopped outside, one on each side of the closed door. The other two, who walked me into the room, had handkerchiefs over their mouths and noses, and tears streaming down their faces.

A thing came toward us. It could have been a praying mantis, if they grew them that big and gave them human eyes. It chittered disapprovingly at my captors.

"Is keep out here," it told them. "Not for breathing. Rendering about to commence. Go away. Leave this place. *Tch-tch-tch!* Not for your kind in here now."

And then the smoke cleared for a moment, and I saw them on the other side of the cauldron. My heart leapt. They were trussed, hand and foot, and they were on the ground, like rabbits ready for the pot. My teammates.

I could see at a glance that they were all there: Jai, Jakon, J/O, Jo and Josef. And they were conscious. They looked haggard and hopeless. I didn't know how long it had been for them—days? weeks? months?—but it didn't look like it had been a pleasant stay. All of them had lost weight, even little J/O.

They also didn't look surprised to see me. Maybe word had already filtered down that I'd been captured, or maybe they'd just been expecting it. I'd screwed up enough so far; it was kind of obvious that I'd do it again, one final time. They simply looked at me, and the resignation in their faces cut me to the bone.

What made it worse was that I knew they were right. This wasn't the kind of place that you made a dramatic last-minute escape from. This was the kind of place you died in.

Painfully, slowly and full of regret.

One of my escorts let go of me, took a step forward and said, "Got another one to pop in the pot. Lord Dogknife's orders."

There was a belch of sulphur from the flames below the pot, and my other guard took his hands off me to wipe his streaming eyes.

And that was when I sprang into action.

Well, "sprang" isn't quite the word, but it sounds better than "stumbled and kicked," which is what I did. I stumbled forward, and then I kicked, as hard as I could, at the nearest strut of the tripod holding up the giant cauldron.

I wish I could tell you that I had a brilliant plan. I didn't. I just wanted to buy us a little more time. Or do *something*, anyway.

It was like being in a car accident. Everything happened so slowly, then . . .

The leg of the tripod leaned over, out of position.

I could see my guards, coughing and spluttering, coming for me.

The cauldron began to tip.

The toad thing, who had been feeding the various salts into the flames so carefully, dropped the whole tray of powders into the flames as it sprang back out of the way, straight into the nearest guard, who cursed and stumbled backward into the mantid.

I threw myself over to the side of the cauldron as the powders in the flame erupted like a tiny fireworks display. . . .

And slowly, majestically and unstoppably, the cauldron tipped over.

I will never forget the guard raising his hand, as if to keep the cauldron from falling onto him, and the way it just kept falling. I will never forget the molten stuff in the cauldron splashing and pouring out, nor the screams of the creatures as it touched them. That stuff burned, and it kept on burning. Even through bone.

I was choking. I could hardly breathe. The world was swimming around me, and I could feel the tears running down my cheeks. But I kept going.

I picked up what looked like a boning knife from the floor, and I started to cut my teammates' ropes. I picked Jo first, cutting the ropes that bound her wings, then slitting her gag.

"Thanks," she said.

"Wings," I gasped. "Air. Fan us. Air." I moved on to Jakon.

Jo nodded, then stretched her wings and began to flap them, blowing the choking smoke away from us. There was fresh air coming up through the grill—to feed the fire, I guess—and I gulped it, and wiped my eyes, and kept sawing away at the ropes with the knife. Jakon seemed the liveliest of the team, wriggling and moving in her bonds, and she sprang out, snapping the last of the ropes before I'd even finished.

Then she bared her teeth, growled deeply and sprang at me.

I ducked.

Over my head went the wolf girl, tearing into the mantid, which had been coming for me with a cleaver.

With one angry blow she tore its head off, and the body stumbled about, cleaver waving, blind and angry.

I freed Josef next. The ropes that bound him were thick as ship's cables. I loosed his hands, then handed him a knife and told him to do the ones around his feet himself. He rubbed his hands and grimaced, and then cut through his ropes twice as fast as I had done.

Out of the corner of my eye I could see Jakon guarding us like a wolf guarding her cubs, every hair on her head standing straight up, her teeth bared, and Jo, who was still fanning the air, and who had also grabbed a pike from the wall and was jabbing it at any of the nasties who dared to approach her. Not that many of them did. Most of them were huddling in the corner and trying to keep away from the flaming molten river between us and them.

I freed Jai.

He rolled uncomfortably on the ground. "I'm paresthetic," he said, "all pins and needles. Also, I am deeply, utterly beholden to you."

"No problem," I said.

I slit J/O's gag. "Typical," he said. "Leave me to last. Just because I'm the smallest. I suppose you think that's fair. *Mmmph, mmph mph mmmmmmmph.*" He said that last because I'd put the gag back into his mouth.

"Actually," I said, "what you mean is, 'Thank you.' And if you don't say it, I'm going to forget about cutting you loose and leave you here, accidentally on purpose."

I took the gag out. His eyes looked very big and very round.

"Thank you," he said in a small voice, "for coming back. For setting me loose. Thank you."

"You're welcome," I told him. "Don't mention it." And I cut his feet loose and then his hands.

The smoke was beginning to thin now, and the fire was behaving more like a fire and less like Vesuvius. My teammates and I gathered together. I guessed there must be strong fireproofing spells on the rendering room—the flames weren't spreading to the walls or to the ceiling or floor. And they were starting to go down.

"We must perforce perambulate with all possible dispatch," Jai said. "No doubt our sudden revolutionary upheaval has activated numerous alarm cantrips."

"We won't be able to fight our way through the entire ship," Jo said, "but dying in battle is better than dying in a pot of boiling blood."

"We are not dying in battle or in blood," I told her. "It's not going to happen. But the only door is on the other side of the fire."

"Actually," said J/O with a certain smug joy at the edge of his voice, "there's a concealed door just down there. I saw one of the squirmy things come out of it when they brought us in."

"Good eye," I said. "But how do we open it? It'll be protected by spells or something like that, won't it?"

On the other side of the flames, the guard, who was still standing, and the various creepies were regrouping and staring at us and talking. We didn't have surprise on our side any longer. We had to move, one way or another.

Josef shrugged. Then he spat on his hands, reached down and heaved. The muscles on the side of his neck bulged. He grunted with the strain, and then moved back. The outline of a hatch was visible, where the grill met the wall. He grinned, then he slammed it with his massive foot, hard.

There was now a hatch-sized hole in the wall.

"Spells are one thing," he said. "Brute force is another. Let's go."

Those of us who had no weapons pulled them from the wall of the rendering room. I paused and picked up a small leather sack, filled with some kind of powder, that was hanging on the wall.

"What's that?" asked J/O.

"No idea," I said. "But my guess is it's the stuff they were throwing on the fire. Some kind of gunpowder. It couldn't hurt."

He made a face. "I don't think it's gunpowder. It's some weird magical stuff. Eye of newt or whatever. You'd better leave it here."

That decided me. I thrust the pouch into my pocket, and then we went through the hole, down a narrow passage hardly bigger than a ventilation shaft.

J/O was in the lead, and Jakon brought up the rear. The rest of us did the best we could in the middle, blundering into one another in the dark.

"You took your time," said Jo. I heard feathers rustle as she hunched her wings together.

"I came as soon as I could. What happened to all of you?"

"They took us to a sort of a prison place," said J/O. "We were in individual cells. We weren't allowed to talk to anyone, read or anything. And the food—*yechh*. I found a bug in mine."

"The bugs were the best part," said Jakon. "They didn't even bother to interrogate us. It was pretty obvious we were for the pot." She hesitated, and I sensed her shivering in the dark. "I met Lord Dogknife. He said we'd suffer, that he'd see to it."

I remembered that hideous goblin face smiling at me. "He said the same thing to me," I told them. "It makes for maximum fuel efficiency." I was glad no one could see my face in the dark.

"We hoped you would come back for us," Jo said, "or that

you'd get back to InterWorld and they would send out a search and rescue party. But as the weeks went by and you didn't come, we started to lose hope. And when they took us to HEX Prime and put us on the *Malefic*, I think we all knew we were dead meat."

I briefly explained what had happened—how HEX had used a shadow realm to throw us off the trail and how I'd been mustered out and mind wiped, only to regain my memory, thanks to Hue. Just about the time I finished, J/O said he saw light ahead.

It took another ten minutes of walking before the rest of us saw it—J/O's cybervision was much more sensitive to light than ordinary eyes. But eventually we all came out of the tunnel and into the light, and stared down in awe.

We stood on a mezzanine overlooking what had to be the engine room. I'm still not sure how the *Malefic* flew, but if sheer size counts for anything, the engines had power to spare. They were gigantic. The chamber must have taken up the entire lowest level of the ship. Below us were enormous pistons and valves and rotating gears as big as the city rotunda back in Greenville. Steam shot from huge petcocks, and bus bars slammed together with deafening clangs. It reminded me of pictures I'd seen of the engine rooms on old ocean liners like *Titanic*—only those ships didn't have trolls and goblins tending the machinery.

Then Jai touched my arm and pointed to one side. I

turned, and saw what was powering the engines: a huge wall stacked floor to ceiling with what looked like large apothecary jars, or old-fashioned apple cider bottles, made of thick glass. In each of them was what looked like the glow of a firefly, without the firefly—a gentle luminescence that pulsed slightly in rhythm with the pounding machinery. They came in many colors, from firefly green to fluorescent yellows and oranges and eye-popping purples. A tube went up from the top of each jar to a huge pipe in the ceiling, which went down to the center of the engine.

"These are our brothers," whispered Jai.

"And sisters," added Jakon.

I touched the side of one cold jar with my hand, and it glowed a bright orange at my touch, as if it recognized me. Inside these jars was the fuel that drove the dreadnought: the essence of Walkers like me, disembodied, bottled and enslaved.

The glass, or whatever material it was, seemed to vibrate slightly. All I could think of was that scene from a hundred different horror movies, in which someone who's been possessed has a moment of sanity and pleads, "Kill me!"

"That could have been us," growled Jakon.

"It still could be," rumbled Josef.

"It's an abomination," said Jo. "I wish there was something we could do for them."

"There is," said Jai. His mouth was an angry line. Jai had

always seemed so gentle. Now I could feel his anger in the air, like static before a thunderstorm.

He furrowed his brow and stared at a glass jar far above us. I thought I saw it shiver. Jai concentrated harder, closing his eyes—and the jar shattered, exploding with a *pop!* like a firecracker. A light hung in the air where the jar had been, edging nervously about, as if it were unused to freedom.

I looked at the others. We were all in agreement.

The iron thing I'd taken from the rendering room looked something like a poleax, with a blade on one side of the head and a blunt hammer on the other. The right tool for the job, as Dad would say.

I stepped forward. I yelled as I swung it—a savage cry that almost drowned out the sound of it smashing into the jars. About five of them shattered with the first blow. The glows within those bottles flared brightly, enough to leave an afterimage.

The rest of the team went at it with just as much enthusiasm and more. The air was filled with flying glass and strobing lights. I stole a glance over my shoulder. Pandemonium was taking place down in the engine room. The huge pistons were stuttering, pumping out of sequence or stopping completely. Steam was venting more and more furiously from various valves and exploding from pipes. Goblins, gremlins and other kinds of fairy-tale rejects were scrambling around like rats on hot tin, panicked.

The great machine was stopping.

At the moment, I didn't care. I just cared about freeing the souls of all the different versions of me from their glass prisons. As each bottle smashed and popped, I felt brighter and stronger. More complete.

More *alive*.

I realized that Josef was actually singing as he smashed. He had a high, tenor voice. It seemed to be a song about an old woman, her nose and a number of herrings; and it made me wonder what kind of world he came from.

And then I noticed something.

The lights weren't fading, once they were freed from their bottles. They were hanging there in space. If anything they were getting brighter, pulsing their firefly colors. They were collecting just above our heads. I didn't know if what was left of them could appreciate what we did or not. It didn't matter. *We* knew.

Jakon smashed the final bottle; and it popped and cracked, and the soul inside was freed, and rose to hang with the others.

Everything was electric. I mean that literally—it felt like the air was supercharged: Every hair on my body was standing on end. I was scared to touch anything in case I might somehow zap it to cinders. And the lights hung above us.

Maybe we imagined it, but if we did, we all imagined it at the same time. I like to think that because, on some very real level, they were us—or they had once been us, before they were slaughtered and used to power a ship between the worlds—that what they thought spilled over to us.

They thought *revenge*. They thought *destruction*. They thought *hate*. And, observing us, they pulsed something that felt a whole lot like *thank you*.

The soul lights began to glow more and more brightly, so brightly that all of us except Jakon and J/O were forced to look away. And then they moved, and I thought I could hear the wind whistling as they went.

Down by the engines the trolls and goblins were bolting everywhere in terror and panic. They didn't have a chance in hell—literally. As the lights hit them, each one of them burst into something that looked like an X-ray image that flared and then was gone.

The lights reached the engines.

I suppose that I'd hate those engines, too, if I'd been driving them with everything I had, everything I *was*. When the sparks reached the engines, they vanished. It was like the steel and iron and bronze and steam had somehow sucked them in.

"What are they doing?" asked J/O.

"Hush," said Jakon.

"I hate to go all practical and everything," I said, "but Lord Dogknife and Lady Indigo are probably sending more troops down that tunnel after us right about now. In fact, I'm surprised they haven't—"

"Quiet," said Jo. "I think she's going to blow."

And then she blew, and it was wonderful. It was like a light show and a fireworks show and the destruction of Sauron's tower . . . everything you could imagine it could be. The *Malefic*'s engines seemed to start to *dissolve* in light, in flame, in magic; and then, with a rumble that grew into a prehistoric roar, they *blew*.

"That is indubitably an supereminent conflagration," sighed Jai, a huge smile on his face.

"Nice," agreed Josef. "Pretty."

If there was a warranty on the *Malefic*'s engines, it had been well and truly voided now.

Then, as the dust settled, I felt it with my mind. Where the engines had been below us was now a portal to the In-Between: the biggest gate I'd ever encountered.

"There's a gate down there," I said. "I suppose that the whole fabric of space-time must have been under pressure from the engines. Now the engines are gone, they've left a place we can get through."

Jakon growled, in the back of her throat. "Then we'd better do it fast," she said. "I can smell a whole battalion of the scum coming up behind us, down that passage."

"And besides," said Jai, "I think our friends have only just begun to fight."

I looked, and he was right, because the soul sparks were

now even brighter now, as they rose from the place where the engines had been and made their way through the ceiling to the floor above.

"I can fly J/O down there," said Jo. "Jai can teleport himself and probably carry Joey or Jakon. But Josef's a bit big to be carried."

Josef shrugged. "S'okay," he said. "I can jump."

We all knew he could survive it. My only concern was him maybe going right through the floor and into the Nowhere-at-All.

But there was no time for hesitation or second thoughts. I could hear the clatter of boots in the tunnel, coming toward us. We'd have to move. And the portal wasn't going to be there for very long: It felt unstable.

There was only one problem.

"Guys," I said. "Lord Dogknife's got Hue. And I'm not leaving without him. He's saved my life more than once. He's saved all of us. I'm sorry. I'll get you through the gate if you want. But I'm staying for Hue."

And then the first of the soldiers came through the door.

CHAPTER EIGHTEEN

There was a rumble from above us, and a big section of a pipe broke free and crashed down. It didn't come anywhere near us. I wondered what the freed souls were doing to the rest of the ship. Then I turned back to the disaster at hand.

As the first soldier came through the opening, Josef picked him up, like a kid picking up an action figure, and dropped him over the side of the mezzanine to the floor below. He screamed a little on the way down.

"So," said Jai to me, "you are declining to accompany us home in order to foolishly squander your life in attempting to rescue your pet multidimensional life-form from . . ." He trailed off as another handful of astoundingly ugly soldier critters came through the corridor and were respectively picked up, teleported and blown over the rail to drop onto the floor below us in varying stages of dead.

"Yes," I said. "I suppose I am."

He sighed. Then he looked at Jo.

"Sounds good to me," she said.

"Me, too," said Josef. "I'm in—hey, not so fast!" and he tossed one of the soldiers back down the corridor, tumbling men like ninepins.

"Say please," J/O said.

"What?"

"Say please and I'll help get your pet back."

"Please," I said. I swung the poleax, and another soldier thing fell screaming. Then we waited, but no more came through the corridor. They seemed to have given up on that idea.

"We'd better to hurry," said Jakon. "I don't think this ship is going to be here for much longer. And Lord Dogknife is going to be getting off before it goes. I know his kind."

I said, "Nobody's mentioned the real problem yet."

Jai smiled. "Which real problem in particular might that be?"

"We're on the bottom of the ship. We need to get to the top deck. And the quickest way is probably back through the corridor we just came down."

"Not necessarily," said Jo. She pointed down. "Look over there."

There was a grand door to the engine room, a huge thing made of brass, and it was opening now, slowly, being wheeled or winched, screeching and complaining like the Wicked Witch of the West as it did so. Once it was open a small phalanx of HEX soldiers marched through it and formed lines. They made no move to attack, however. They simply formed a solid wall of flesh and weapons, facing us.

For a tense moment no one moved. Then the HEX soldiers split ranks, to reveal a single man standing there. A man whose naked flesh crawled with nightmares.

"Hello, Scarabus," I shouted, trying to sound confident, although my skin felt like it was crawling just as much as his. "Enjoying the cruise? There's gonna be shuffleboard and bingo later."

"I felt from the start that Neville and the Lady Indigo underestimated you, boy," he called back up to me. "I would have been happy to have been proven wrong." He put his hand on the small image of a scimitar tattooed on his left bicep, and suddenly there was a real scimitar, the oiled blade gleaming wickedly, in his right hand.

"You've destroyed the *Malefic*," he said. "The conquest of the Lorimare worlds has failed. Lord Dogknife intends to deal with you all personally. Believe me, every one of you will wish you had gone in the pot instead."

Good, I thought. Lord Dogknife was still on the ship.

Jai tapped me on the shoulder. I moved out of the way. Jai looked down at Scarabus and said, without raising his voice, but clearly audible across the whole huge hall, "We have a deal to offer you. To all of you."

"I don't think you're in any position to make deals." Scarabus slashed his scimitar through the air.

"But we are," said Jai. "One of us will fight you. If our champion wins, you alone will escort us up to Lord

Dogknife as free folk. If our champion loses, you may march us to Lord Dogknife as your prisoners."

Scarabus stared at Jai for a heartbeat, and then he began to laugh. It was obvious why. From his point of view, whether we won or lost, we wound up in Lord Dogknife's clutches. I couldn't see that it made much difference either. One could call Lord Dogknife a lot of things, most of them uncomplimentary and none in his presence, but "stupid" wasn't one of them.

"Bring on your champion!" Scarabus shouted.

Jai shook his head. "I need you, and all your men to swear not to harm us, if our champion wins."

The soldiers looked at Scarabus. He nodded. "I so swear!" he shouted. "And I!" "And I!" repeated the soldiers one by one. They looked vastly entertained.

"I'm ready," I said to Jai. I knew he had a plan, and I just hoped I'd learn what it was in time.

"You?" said Jakon with scorn in her voice. "Let me take him on. I'll rip out his throat."

"Excuse me?" said Josef. "Biggest? Strongest? Come on, guys, do the multidimensional math."

"It's not a matter of strength," said J/O. "It's a matter of swordsmanship. Has anyone here ever gone up against a scimitar?" None of us answered. "Well," he continued, "I was an Olympic level fencer. And I've done historical reen-actment sword fighting, with broadswords and short swords—and scimitars."

"This is a magical location," said Jai. "Strong magic. You are already weakened, and you are the smallest of us, J/O. This world does not recognize your abilities."

"It's not a matter of nanocircuitry and augmented reflexes," said J/O. "It's a matter of skill. I can do it."

They all looked at me, and I looked at Jai. He nodded.

J/O looked as smug as a cyborg face can look. "Jo, can you fly me down there?"

She nodded.

"Ask them for a sword, then."

I shrugged. "Hey!" I called. "Have you got a spare sword, for our champion?"

One of the soldiers produced a sword, took a few steps forward, put it down on the floor, stepped back again. The laughter increased.

"Thank you," I said. "Enjoy the show. Remember to tip your waiter."

Jo picked J/O up then, and she flew down him to the floor. He picked up the sword—which was almost as long as he was—and bowed low to Scarabus.

The soldiers laughed louder still. If it were possible to laugh oneself to death, we would have already won. Scarabus looked up at us. "What?" he asked. "Are you sending me the smallest child in the hope that I'll be merciful?" He grinned widely. "I shall *not* be merciful!" he said. And then he raised his scimitar and charged.

He was good. He was very, very good.

Trouble was, it was obvious to all of us—even him, even the soldiers—that J/O was better. From the first moment their blades crossed, he was faster. *Way* faster. He seemed to know exactly where Scarabus's scimitar was at any point in the fight, and he was always somewhere else.

The main thing I remember is just how loud the fight was. Every time the blades clashed, the room rang with the sound of metal banging metal. I can still hear it.

Pretty soon Scarabus seemed to abandon the whole idea of clever sword fighting and tried to win by taking advantage of his size and strength, slamming J/O with great blows that cyber-me barely seemed able to parry or block.

Then J/O tripped, and Scarabus lunged, bringing down the blade with all his might, shouting in triumph—and J/O moved, quick as thought, to one side, raising his sword as he did so.

The tattooed man impaled himself on J/O's sword.

Scarabus's victory cry was cut off. He didn't scream—he didn't make a sound. He just gripped the metal shaft and stared at J/O in amazement.

Then he fell to the floor—and all hell *really* broke loose.

His skin *boiled*. It was as if all the tattoos had been imprisoned there in his flesh somehow, and were released by his death. Monsters, demons, things for which I had no name—

they all rose up and away from him, expanding and solidifying—

And then they shuddered and froze in mid-flight for an instant.

Then—it was like watching a film run backward. The tats were sucked back down in a whirlpool of ink and form, and in seconds were safely in his skin once more. Scarabus pushed himself up to his elbow, coughed red blood and wiped it away with one illustrated hand. "You just cost me a life," he said to J/O. "A *life*! You little monster."

From his place beside me, Jai asked calmly, "Will you accompany us to Lord Dogknife's presence without harming us?"

"I have no choice," said Scarabus. "I swore an oath. There's too much raw magic in the air to go back on it now."

Two soldiers helped him to his feet as Jai, Josef, Jakon and I joined J/O and Scarabus on the floor of the engine room.

"Good job," I said to J/O. I meant it.

He shrugged, but his eyes shone with pleasure.

We started to run, as best we could, up a set of narrow wooden stairs. Every deck we passed showed chaos—people, and things that weren't people, were panicking, running, screaming.

Scarabus cursed us, demanding that we slow down. He was somewhere behind us. We ignored him. The *Malefic* wouldn't hold together much longer.

"More like the *Titanic* than the *Malefic*," I said to Jo, trying to catch my breath. There were a *lot* of stairs.

"*Titanic?*"

"Big ship, from my Earth. Hit an iceberg. Went down. nineteen twelve, thereabouts."

"Oh right," she said. "Like the *King John* disaster."

"Whatever," I said, as a huge chunk of ship fell apart to one side of us, and went tumbling off into the Nowhere-at-All.

We kept running up steps and along corridors and up more steps. And then we were there, outside the auditorium, the place where I had seen Lord Dogknife last, an hour or so earlier.

And I stopped.

The others stopped, too. "Hey," said Josef. "Something wrong?"

"He's in there," I said. "Don't ask me how I know."

Jai nodded. "Good enough," he said.

Josef kicked down the door and we all went in.

CHAPTER NINETEEN

The room was dark, the only source of light a firefly-green glow on the other side of the hall. We waited near the door, none of us willing to go farther in, letting our eyes adjust to the blackness.

And then a honeyed snarl whispered from the gloom. "Hello, children," said Lord Dogknife. "Come to gloat, have we?"

We edged into the room. There was a black shape, outlined against the green glow.

"No," said Jo. "We don't gloat. We're the good guys."

There was a grunt. The glow light grew slightly brighter.

Now I could see what it was. The Walker souls, the ones from the jars, were hanging in the air, pressed together like an enormous swarm of bees. And facing them, with his hands plunged deep into the center of the swarm, was Lord Dogknife. He seemed to be holding the souls in place, but the effort was obviously costing him energy and effort. He was wheezing even more than usual, and he did not turn to look at us as we came closer.

"You creatures have caused me a great deal of trouble,"

gasped Lord Dogknife. "Freeing these ghosts has cost me my ship, *and* the Lorimare invasion."

"And FrostNight?" I asked.

He turned and looked at us then, and the swarm pulsed more brightly. One tiny light parted from the whole and skimmed toward Dogknife's face, raking down his cheek. Dogknife almost seemed to stumble, and then pulled himself back to his feet and growled, "No. FrostNight will continue on schedule, whatever happens to me."

There was a shudder and a crash as something below us fell apart. That was happening more and more lately.

"Why are you here?" I asked. "Shouldn't you be in a lifeboat or something by now?"

It was like the bellow of a bull or the growl of a tiger. "Cannot you see, boy? This ridiculous simmered-up ball of spirits has me caught." He groaned and heaved, trying, vainly, to pull away. The firefly-green light burned more brightly. It began to spread up his arms, oozing like slow green oil. It made sense. If he'd had me imprisoned in a glass bottle for years—having first had mind-mashing amounts of pain inflicted upon me, to help me "focus"—I know what I would have wanted to do. I would have wanted to hurt him, just like he hurt me. I would have kept him on the ship until it blew or crashed or did whatever sabotaged ships did in the Nowhere-at-All.

Josef touched my shoulder. "Joey? This is your deal.

215

Whatever you're going to do, you need to do it fast."

I nodded. Took a deep breath and walked forward. I faced those eyes, eyes that were the color of cancer, of bile, of venom. I looked into them, even though every cell of my body was telling me to run, and I said, "I want my mudluff back."

His huge hyena face twisted briefly into an expression of amusement. I could see him calculating, realizing that he had something I wanted.

"Ahhhh. You didn't come all the way back here just to witness my death. You want the creature, then?"

"Yes."

A light flashed brightly in the swarm of souls, and Lord Dogknife flinched. "Then get me out of here, and I'll give you your little friend back. But you must free me. Right now I couldn't even get the prism if I wanted to. My hands are somewhat occupied."

"Why should we trust you?" called Jakon.

"You can't trust me. Nor should you—" He paused then, grunted and seemed to concentrate. Then he moaned. It was the closest I ever heard Lord Dogknife come to making a sound of weakness, of pain. I had to admit, it didn't give me as much satisfaction as I might have hoped. Still, I was a long way from feeling sorry for him.

"If you want your pet back, then for the sake of all you hold holy," he said, "*help* me. I will not last much longer. The pain is more than I can bear. And I can bear *much* pain . . ."

I hesitated. "I don't even know if I can help. What if we just took back the prism?"

"Then," he panted, "you would have a prism with an ouroboros imprisoned in it. You need me to open it."

The ship gave a sudden lurch, and suddenly everything was at forty-five degrees. I lost my footing on the slippery wooden floor and slammed against the wall. I rolled out of the way barely in time to avoid Lord Dogknife, who hit the same spot, only a lot harder. He groaned and pulled himself back to his feet.

Tentatively, I put out my hand and pushed into the glowing light.

Hate.

Hate filled my mind.

The desire for revenge.

Each of the spirits, and there were hundreds of them in that swarm, still roiled and reeled and writhed in pain. They were full of hate; hate for the ship, hate for HEX, hate for Lord Dogknife, hate for Lady Indigo; hate was the only thing they had to distract them from the pain.

It was horrible. All over my mind, hundreds of versions of *me* were screaming.

I had to stop it.

"It's over," I told them, hardly knowing what I was saying. "No one's going to hurt you again. You're free. Let go. Move on." I tried to think of good things to back up the thoughts I was sending them. Hot summer days. Warm winter nights by the fire. Thunderstorms. After a while I ran out of commonplace touchy-feely things and concentrated on family memories. The smell of Dad's pipe. The squid's smile. The stone around my neck, the one that my mother gave me before I left.

The stone . . .

For no reason I could name, I reached in my shirt and pulled it out. It hung in my hand, reflecting the flickers and pulses of the souls. And then I noticed something peculiar: The stone wasn't just echoing the lights; it was resonating with them, harmonizing with the flickering colors, somehow. And I could see the firefly lights were changing; beginning to pulse and flare in sync. If it had been sound instead of light, I would have been hearing two contrapuntal melodies that were slowly merging.

They were almost ready to believe me. I knew it, somehow. Almost, but not quite.

"Stop fighting them," I told Dogknife.

"*What?*"

"As long as you're fighting them, they'll keep trying to destroy you. Just stop fighting them and they'll let you go."

"Why"—he gasped—"why should I trust you?"

"We've just been over all that. Now stop fighting them."

And he did. He relaxed every muscle, and I could almost

hear the tension fade. *See?* I told the sparks in my head, barely realizing I wasn't speaking out loud. *Now let it go.*

The light began to glow more and more brightly, filling the room with a blinding radiance. I closed my eyes, screwed them up tightly, but the light filled my head and my mind. I thought I heard something say *good-bye*, but I might have just imagined it. Then the light faded, and Mom's stone went out as well.

The whole room went dark.

"Take it," said Lord Dogknife's voice. Something sharp and cold was pressed into my hand.

"Thanks," I gasped, without thinking.

Something flickered and a nearby candelabra erupted into flames. Lord Dogknife stood next to me. His breath was a pestilence, and the pure hatred gleaming from his eyes could have put the sun out. He bared his teeth, so close that I could see things, like tiny, almost microscopic maggots, crawling on them.

"Do not thank me, boy," that ruined snout whispered. "The next time we meet, I shall chew your face from your skull. I'll floss with your guts. You have cost me so much. So do not—*ever*—thank me."

He put his head on one side, as if he were listening for something, and then he howled loudly, like a maddened wolf.

"My associates are coming," he said.

"Open Hue's prism," I told him, "or I'm calling back the spirits."

His sharp teeth glinted in the candlelight. "You are lying. You cannot do that."

He was right, of course. I couldn't, but he couldn't be sure of that. I cupped the stone pendant in my free hand. "Let's find out," I said.

His red eyes burned into mine, but he was the first to flinch. The prism began to feel ice-cold, like the hull of a space shuttle must. "It will not open completely in my presence," growled Lord Dogknife. He grabbed me then, lifted me off my feet. "So, sadly, you must take your leave, *Walker*."

He threw me, like an Olympic javelin thrower might casually toss a twig. I flew the length of that huge room, hard enough to break half the bones in my body when I hit the far wall. Which, fortunately, didn't happen, because Jo threw herself across my path, using her wings to slow us down. We landed softly on the deck, and an instant later the rest of my team had surrounded me. I got to my feet, and would have fallen again when the deck lurched suddenly, if Jakon hadn't grabbed me. Everything was shuddering now. I could see rivets cracking, and sections of the hull warping.

Dogknife howled again, and the far wall erupted into wood fragments. Something was hanging in the not-space alongside the ship, something that looked like a magic carpet upgraded to a modern day life raft. I could make out

Lady Indigo, Scarabus, Neville and a number of other creatures who might have been HEX bigwigs on it.

Lord Dogknife growled and leapt for the raft, landing on it hard enough to catapult a creature on the edge of the raft screaming, out into the Nowhere-at-All.

And then, like a bad memory, the raft was gone, and the *Malefic* was tearing itself to pieces around us.

"Where's the portal?" shouted Jai.

I was going to tell him it was below us, but then I realized it wasn't below us anymore. It was somewhere to my right, a few hundred yards away. "It's somewhere over there!" I shouted back, pointing.

Around about then, the ceiling started to come down.

We ran.

"*Out!*" bellowed Josef. "Let's head for the deck! It's our only chance!"

"Less talk, more running," said Jakon.

The prism in my hand felt colder. Then it felt wet. It was a strange feeling, familiar, but I couldn't stop to open my hand and look at it. I was running, trying to keep up with the rest of the team.

The prism began to drip from my hand as a liquid. It was ice, I realized with a shock. Nothing more than melting ice. I hoped it hadn't been some kind of trick on Lord Dogknife's part.

A section of the floor started to crumble beneath us. J/O,

Jakon, Jai and Jo made it across to the nearby staircase. Josef and I didn't. Now there was a gap, easily ten feet wide, with flames erupting from it. Flames were spreading along the floor behind us.

"We're never going to get out of here alive," said someone. I think it was me.

The planks beneath me started tumbling away. I stepped back onto what I hoped was more solid footing. It wasn't.

There was nothing but fire beneath me. But before I could fall into it, somebody picked me up, grabbing me by the belt as the deck vanished completely. "Hey," said Jo. "Relax, or I might drop you."

I relaxed. Her wings flapping, she rose above the hole and put me down on an untouched part of the deck. Then she turned back, dropping again to rescue Josef, who was hanging from a spar.

"You okay?" asked Jakon. I nodded. Then I opened my hand, where the prism had been. There was nothing there.

"He tricked me." I said. "He lied."

Jakon grinned. "I don't think so." She pointed above me.

I looked up. Hue hung in the air above me. He was faint and gray, but there nonetheless. I felt relief wash over me. "Hue! You're back! Are you okay?"

A faint blush of pink spread along the mudluff's bubble surface.

"I think she may have been hurt," said Jakon.

222

I wondered about the "she" part, but there was no time to get into something as potentially complicated as that. "The quickest route's through here," I said, pointing at the wall. J/O stepped up and aimed his blaster arm. I didn't see what he did; the smoke had become so thick that I couldn't see, or breath very well either. "Hurry," I said, coughing. Then I saw a flash of scarlet light through my closed eyelids, heard something like *ffzzzhhsstt!!* and suddenly there was fresh air in my face. Someone pushed me forward, and I stumbled out onto the *Malefic's* forward deck.

"There's the gate," said Josef. "Look." You could see it almost a hundred yards away to one side of the ship, glimmering against the strangeness of the Nowhere-at-All. "How do we get there?"

Jai said, "Jo, can you navigate the ether?"

"Can I fly over there?" She hesitated. "I don't know. Probably not."

"This is crazy," growled Jakon. "We're going to die on this stupid ship within sight of a gate."

I looked again at the "hole" in the "sky." It looked smaller, as if we'd drifted farther away. No. We weren't drifting.

The gate was shrinking.

I looked up at Hue. "Hue! Could you get us out of here?"

He pulsed a sad gray. He had obviously been hurt by his time in the prism.

"Okay. Could you get us over to the portal?"

Again, a gloomy gray pulse. No. He couldn't even do that.

"Well, then, could you get *one* of us over to the portal?"

A pause. Than a positive blue spread across Hue's surface.

"Great," said J/O. "So you get to live, and we get to die. That's great. That's just great, by which I mean, it really sucks, in case you were wondering."

"You know," I told him, "I was just starting to like you, after that sword fight. *All* of us are getting out. And the one I want Hue to carry over is Josef."

"Me?" said Josef, his brow creasing.

"That's right," I told him. There was another explosion from below us, and another chunk of the ship dissolved into splinters.

"Quick," I told them, looking around, "we need that rigging over there, and—yes! There's a segment of mast down there. We need it over here."

Jakon grabbed the rigging—it was the size of a couple of bedsheets, a netlike tangle of thumb-thick line—and Jai, with a little effort, levitated one end of the broken mast from under the pile of broken spars and timbers. Jo pulled up with the other, flapping her wings as she did so, and Josef and I pushed it up and over to the spot I had indicated.

I wrapped the rigging around the spar, tying it at the top and the bottom. It wouldn't win any design awards, but it would serve. I hoped.

"Now," I said. "Let's hope that there isn't much inertia in

the Nowhere-at-All. Josef, how's your javelin throwing?"

"Why?"

"Because," I told him, "I want you to throw us at the gate."

They all stared at me with that particular stare reserved for someone you've pinned your last hopes on, only to discover he's utterly mad. "You're crazy," said Jakon. "The moon has taken your mind."

"No," I told her, told all of them. "It's perfectly sensible. We hold on to the rigging, and Josef throws the mast toward the gate. It's still pretty huge, although it's shrinking fast. We hit it, I open it and Hue brings Josef through."

They looked at each other. "It sounds very straightforward that way," said Jo.

"It sounds like worms have eaten your brain," said Jakon.

"Completely cracked," agreed J/O. "Neural systems failure."

"Josef," said Jai. "Do you believe you can throw us that far?"

Josef reached down and hefted the length of mast. It was as long as, although thinner than, a telephone pole. He grunted with the effort, then nodded. "Yeah," he said. "I think so. Maybe."

Jai closed his eyes. He took several deep breaths, as if he were meditating. Then he said, "Very well. It will be as Joey says."

"Hue," I said. "You have to stay here, on deck, and bring Josef over to us once we're on our way. Can you do that?"

There was a green glow from one small bubbly corner.

"How do you know it even understands you?" asked Jo.

"Do you have a better idea?" I asked her. She shook her head.

We pushed the mast over the side of the ship, with the end pointing slightly up and toward the gate, which was pulsating like a holographic nebula in the bleakness a hundred yards to the side of us.

"Let's do it," I told Jo. We all, except Josef, clambered onto the mast, holding tightly to the rigging.

"Okay, Josef. Go for it."

He closed his eyes. He grunted. Then he *pushed*.

Slowly we began to move away from the ship. We were falling, flying, coasting toward the gate, moving through the Nowhere-at-All.

"It's working!" shouted Jakon.

Sir Isaac Newton was the first person (on my Earth, anyway) to explain the laws of motion. It's pretty basic stuff: An object (let's just say, for instance, a length of mast with five young interdimensional commandos hanging from it) if left to itself, will, according to the first law, maintain its condition unchanged; the second law points out that a change in motion means that something (like Josef) has acted on the object; the third states that for every action there is a reaction of exactly the same force in the opposite direction.

The first law, the way I saw it, meant that we should have just kept floating toward the rapidly shrinking gate until we got there. True, there was air, or ether or something that we could breathe, but simple atmospheric friction wouldn't slow us enough to stop before we reached it. So my plan was foolproof, right?

Problem is, as I've said before, there are some places where scientific laws are only opinions, and pretty questionable opinions at that. Where magical potency can be stronger than scientific law. The Nowhere-at-All is one of those places.

And the members of HEX know it.

We were still about thirty feet away from the gate when we stopped. Just stopped, and hung there in space.

And then, from behind us, we heard a voice. A voice as sweet as poisoned candy. A voice that, not too long ago, I would have died to hear a single word of praise from. And from the looks on the others' faces, I knew they had once felt the same way.

"No, Joey Harker," the voice said. "No last-minute escape for you."

As one, the five of us, as well as Josef, back on the *Malefic*, turned—

to face Lady Indigo.

CHAPTER TWENTY

She hung in midair, between us and the *Malefic* but to one side, one arm still uplifted, still poised from casting whatever spell she'd cast to stop us. As she spoke, she lifted her other arm and began to float away from the *Malefic* and toward us. "I congratulate you, Joey Harker," she said as she came. "You've done what no one thought possible. You've destroyed the *Malefic* and its mission. Lord Dogknife has already returned to HEX Prime. He has charged me with bringing you to him. I look forward to doing so, believe me. With his conquest of the Lorimare worlds aborted, he has only his thoughts of revenge on you to occupy his time."

She landed on the edge of the mast and started to trace in the air the luminous path of that same sigil she had used on me so long ago, back in one of the countless alternate Greenvilles. As she gestured, she began to speak the Word that would put all six of us in her thrall once again.

I knew I had to do something, or it would all be over. With their mission of conquest destroyed, there would be nothing to stop Lord Dogknife from using all the skill and knowledge he possessed to tear the secret of InterWorld from our minds. If Lady Indigo completed that spell, it was all over, for *everyone*. Worlds without end.

But I didn't know how to stop her. A glance at my teammates showed me that they were already falling under her geas—their eyes were turning glassy, their muscles stiffening. And I could feel her will nibbling at the corners of my mind as well, seductively whispering how easy and *right* it would be to do whatever she told me . . .

Her spell was almost complete. The Word, the Sound of it, reverberated in the air, pulsing in time with the glowing Sign. I felt my hands rising, beginning to shape a gesture of obeisance to her, to Lord Dogknife, to HEX. . . .

I had to distract her somehow. I looked around for something to throw at her, to break her concentration. I shoved my left hand into my pocket, knowing that it would be futile—and my fist closed around the pouch of powder.

I barely stopped to think. Instead, I just acted—I pulled the pouch from my pocket and I threw it at her.

I didn't know what would happen—if anything. It was a gesture of desperation, pure and simple. As I said, the most I hoped to accomplish was to momentarily break her concentration.

But it did far more than that.

When the pouch struck her it *evaporated*, releasing strange crimson powder as it did so.

The red powder swirled around Lady Indigo, enveloping

her in a miniature whirlwind. She looked astonished—and then afraid. She moved her arms in a warding gesture, opened her mouth to speak a negating spell, but no sound came out. The powder swirled faster and faster, and I could feel the potency of her geas lessening. I glanced at the others, and saw they were coming out of it as well.

What meant we had one chance—and only one—for escape.

The gate had been about a hundred feet long in the engine room. It was about fifty feet long when we set out. Now it was starting to evaporate into nothingness.

"Jo!" I called. "Start flapping! And, Jai—can you levitate us toward the portal?"

"I'm not entirely certain," he admitted.

"Be certain," I said. "Give it your best shot."

As for me, I concentrated on the gate. I'm a Walker, after all. I probed, and I pushed. I reached out with my mind. And, with everything at my disposal, I held that gate open.

And slowly, oh so horribly, *horribly* slowly, like a train moving through a small Southern town on a hot summer day, the mast began to move toward the gate.

"It's working!" shouted J/O.

I threw a quick glance at Lady Indigo, reassuring myself that she wouldn't continue to be a problem. It didn't look like she would. There were flashes of light within the crimson whirlwind now, and each one seemed to illuminate the lady from within, as if her flesh had become momentarily translucent, exposing the bones. She was writhing now as if in agony, her mouth open in a scream—a scream that no one could hear.

But the gate was closing, and it was all I could do to keep it open. "J/O! Jakon!" I called. "Help me! We have to keep the gate open!"

I felt their minds—their strength—push with mine, as the gate continued to shrink and fade.

We weren't going to make it in time. We weren't—

The *Malefic* blew up.

It was a huge, black, greasy cloud of an explosion, mushrooming in all directions. I think that if it had happened in the Static, or on a world where science worked better, the shock wave would have killed us. As it was, I felt a great hammering blast of superheated air that sent the mast, with us clinging to it, surging toward the portal—and through it!

Easy as a key turning in a lock, we slipped through the portal into the welcoming madness of the In-Between.

The mast and the rigging evaporated into things that scuttled, spiderlike, into wild, cartoony snarls of grapefruit scent. I glanced back through the narrowing slit of the portal. The Lady Indigo—or what was left of her—was nowhere to be seen. Then the portal blinked out. To this day I don't know what happened to her.

"What about Josef? And Hue?" asked Jo.

There was a fizzing noise, and a burst of emerald sparks, and Josef dropped from the sky in front of us, surrounded by a thin bubble shape, which shrank as we looked at it. It came toward me and settled in the craziness, bobbing like a balloon in a spring breeze.

"I'm here," said Josef. "Let's go home."

Home? I had a pang, as I thought of my mom, my dad, my brother and sister. Places and people I'd probably never see again. I reached up my hand and touched the stone Mom had given me, on my last night there. *You're doing the right thing*, she said in my memory.

Thanks, Mom, I thought, and the pang eased, even if it would never entirely go away.

Then I thought of my home. My new home.

$$\{IW\}:=\Omega/\infty$$

would take us back there, wherever it was hiding.

I Walked, and the rest of my team followed.

CHAPTER TWENTY-ONE

We were all there in the Old Man's outer office: Jai, Josef, Jo, Jakon, J/O and me. We'd been waiting there for almost an hour. The summons had arrived just before breakfast, and we'd come straight down. And then we'd waited.

And waited.

Finally, there was a buzz from the inner office. The Old Man's assistant went inside, then came back out. She walked over to me.

"He wants to talk to you first," she said. "You others wait out here."

I grinned at my friends as I went in. If I didn't feel ten feet tall it was probably because I felt fifteen feet tall. Make that twenty feet tall. I mean, I may not have been part of InterWorld for long, but I—we—had done something pretty amazing. Six of us had taken out a HEX invasion fleet. We'd destroyed the *Malefic*. A dozen worlds, at least, would retain their freedom, thanks to us.

I'm not one to brag, but that's the kind of thing that gets medals.

I wondered what I'd say if he pinned a medal on me. Would

I simply say "Thank you" or would I say something about it being an honor and how I had only done what anyone would have done? Would I babble embarrassingly like those actors who win Oscars . . . or would I say nothing at all?

I couldn't wait to find out.

And what about promotion? Let's face it—I'd make a great team leader. I raised my head slightly, sticking out my chin. True officer material.

Nothing had changed in the Old Man's office. There was the big desk that filled most of the room, still papers, folders, disks, everywhere in piles and heaps. And sitting at the desk was the Old Man, making notes. He didn't seem to notice me when I walked in, so I stood there.

I stood there for a couple of minutes. Finally he closed the file in front of him and looked up.

"Ah. Joey Harker."

"Yes, sir." I tried to sound humble. It wasn't easy.

"I've read your debrief, Joey. There was one thing I was not clear on. Exactly what was the stimulus that returned your memory?"

"My memory?" His question caught me by surprise. "It was the soap bubble, sir. It reminded me of Hue, and with Hue it seemed like everything else just came back."

He nodded and made a note on the report.

"We'll need to take that into account for future amnesiac conditioning," he said. "There's a lot we don't know about mudluffs. For now, you will be permitted to keep the creature with you in the base. This permission may be rescinded at any time."

His LED eye glinted. He made another note.

I stood there. He carried on writing. I wondered if he had forgotten I was there.

This wasn't going exactly the way I'd pictured it.

"Sir?"

He looked up.

"I was wondering . . . well, I thought, maybe we would get some kind of . . . I mean, well, we blew up the *Malefic*, and . . ."

I trailed off. Definitely *not* going the way I'd pictured it.

He sighed. It was a long sigh, weary and worldly-wise. The kind of sigh you could picture God heaving after six days of hard work and looking forward to some serious cosmic R&R, only to be handed a report by an angel concerning a problem with someone eating an apple.

Then he called, "Send the rest of them in."

Everyone walked into his office, shuffling around to make room.

He looked us over. I found myself very aware that he was sitting down, while we were standing. It felt the other way around. It felt like he was looming over us.

Josef, Jo and Jakon all looked pleased with themselves. J/O had a grin spread like peanut butter over his face. The only one who didn't look absolutely thrilled was Jai.

"Well," said the Old Man. "Joey seems to be of the opinion that you six ought to get some kind of medal, or at least some kind of formal recognition for the stellar work that you did. Does anyone here share his opinion?"

"Yes, sir," said J/O. "Did he tell you how I beat Scarabus in the sword fight? We *rocked*."

The others murmured agreement or just nodded.

The Old Man nodded. Then he looked at Jai. "Well?" he said.

"I think we did accomplish a remarkable thing, sir."

The Old Man's eye glittered.

"Oh you do, do you?" he asked.

Then he took a deep breath, and he began.

He told us what he thought of a team who couldn't even accomplish a simple training mission without a disaster. He told us that everything we had accomplished had been due to plain dumb luck. That we'd broken every rule in the book and a few they had never thought to put into any book of rules or book of just plain common sense. He said that if there were any justice in any of the myriad worlds we would all have been rendered down and put in bottles. That we had been overconfident, foolish, ignorant. That we'd taken idiot chances. He said that we should never have gotten into the trouble we'd gotten into. That, having gotten into it, we should have come home *immediately*. . . .

It went on like that for a while.

He didn't raise his voice during any of this. He didn't have to.

I'd walked in twenty feet high, and by the time he had finished I felt mouse height. A crippled, stoop-shouldered mouse. The runt of the litter.

When he finished, the silence was thick enough to fill an ocean, with enough left over for a few great lakes and an inland sea. He looked from one of us to the next in silence. We concentrated very hard on not looking at him—or one another.

And then he said, "Still, as teams go, I think you six may have potential. Well done. Dismissed."

And we shuffled out of there, not meeting one another's eyes.

We stood in the parade ground, all in a clump. The sun was halfway up the sky, and a chilly wind blew across Base Town. The perpetually floating city was drifting over a dense forest that looked like it went on for leagues and probably did. We passed by a clearing, and a creature resembling an overgrown rhinoceros with two side-by-side horns looked up at us.

I think we were in shock.

Hue was twisting slowly in the air about thirty feet up. When he noticed us, he drifted down until he was floating a foot above my right shoulder.

Someone had to say something, but no one wanted to be the first.

Finally, Josef shook his head. "What *happened* in there?" he asked.

Jai grinned suddenly, showing perfect white teeth. "He said we were a team."

There was a pause.

"And he said we have *potential*," said Jakon proudly.

"He said I could keep Hue," I told them.

"Then we're seven in the team," said Jo thoughtfully, spreading her wings against the morning sunlight. "Not six. And he said 'well done,' didn't he? The Old Man said 'well done.' To *us*."

"You hear that?" I asked Hue. "You're part of the team, too." Hue undulated slowly, satisfied oranges and crimsons chasing themselves across his soap-bubble surface. I had no idea whether he understood any of this or not. But I'm pretty sure that he did.

"I still think we rock," said J/O. "And, anyway, we have potential. Who needs medals? I'd rather have potential than medals any day."

"I wonder if there's any breakfast left," said Josef. "I'm starving."

We were all starving, except maybe Hue. So we went to breakfast.

We had almost finished eating when the alarm bells went off. We ran to the bulletin screen at the back of the mess hall and watched images shift and form on it.

"There's a team in trouble," Josef said. "A Binary attack on the Rimworld coalition. It's Jerzy and J'r'ohoho."

The Old Man's voice blared over a loudspeaker: "Joey Harker, assemble your team for immediate action."

I looked at my team. They were ready. So was I.

The balance must be maintained.

I concentrated—and the In-Between bloomed before us.

We Walked.

AFTERWORD

Michael and Neil first started talking about *InterWorld* in about 1995, when Michael was making adventure cartoon serials at DreamWorks and Neil was in London working on the *Neverwhere* TV series. We thought it would make a fun television adventure. Then, as the nineties went on, we started trying to explain our idea to people, telling them about an organization entirely comprised of dozens of Jo/e/y Harkers, trying to preserve the balance between magic and science across an infinite number of possible realities, and we would watch their eyes glaze over. There were ideas you could get across to the kind of people who make television, we decided, and there were ideas you couldn't. Then, as the nineties came to an end, one of us had an idea: Why didn't we write it as a novel? If we just told the story, simply and easily, then even a television executive would be able to understand it. So one snowy day Michael came up to Neil's part of the world, carrying a computer, and while the winter weather howled we wrote this book.

Soon we learned that television executives don't read books either, and we sighed and went about our lives.

InterWorld sat in the darkness for some years, but when, recently, we showed it to people, the people we showed it to thought other people might like to read it. So we brought it out of the darkness and polished it up. We hope you enjoyed it.

—*Neil Gaiman and Michael Reaves*

2007